phobic

s. a. nicola

Mystic Cow Media, USA

ISBN: 0615563805
ISBN-13: 978-0615563800

Agoraphobia

A fear of open spaces, crowds, or anywhere outside of a self-defined "safe" area.

CHAPTER 1

Anna could feel her eyes twitch as the blue pickup approached. She stared at the blood-red gashes of rust around the wheel wells and dug her feet firmly in place on the gravel driveway as if she were bracing herself for an impact. She hated this moment every week, and this time she was sure she wouldn't make it. This time she would be pushed too far, and she would lose control. Probably, she would die.

Dirt skirted around the old Ford as it stopped about ten yards short of turning up the long driveway. Anna twisted a strand of her sandy-blonde hair around her finger, waiting for the truck to drive closer. It didn't. She motioned for the truck to drive in further, but instead the engine idled and died.

"Why don't you pull on up here?" Anna called out.

"No way, no how," Jim Yoder, her father, called back as he stepped out of the pickup. He took off his tattered McCurdy Seeds baseball cap and wiped his forehead, revealing his stark white hair. "This truck isn't coming up there. You'll have to come down here."

"It's gotten real hot today, hasn't it?" Anna asked as she slowly began making her way down the driveway. Her father answered, but she couldn't hear. All she could hear was the rhythm of her feet crunching under the gravel, as if the driveway itself was telling her, *"Go-no furth-er. Go-no furth-er. Go-no furth-er. Go-no furth-er."* The sound of thunder rolled in the distance. She stopped.

"Hurry up, now. I want to get home before the rain comes in." Jim drummed his fingers on the cab of his truck.

"Probably just heat thunder," Anna said. She forced herself forward.

"You're probably right," her dad said as he looked skyward. "Pick up the pace, Anna."

"Go-no-furth-er. Go-no furth-er. Go-no furth-er. Go-no furth-er." Anna's eyes twitched again as she neared the end of the driveway. Her heart pumped as if she had gone fifty miles instead of fifty feet. She stopped and held her arms out in front of her.

"Okay," she said. She knew her wrists and hands had extended over the border, the line where the gravel spilled out into the dirt of the road. She hated it.

"Your groceries are in the back of the truck," Jim said. "Why don't you help out your old man and come get them?"

Anna was frozen, unable to say anything. She felt her mouth curving into a hard frown. Her eyes stared forward. Her hands burned as if the air on the other side of the driveway was toxic. She had gone too far. If something happened, she'd never make it all the way back to the house. The heat of the late summer air combined with the low roar of distant thunder made the air heavy and oppressive.

"I need the bags," was all she managed to say. He'd be mad, he'd be disappointed, but at least she wouldn't have to step off the driveway. Off the driveway might as well be off the edge of the world.

She could hear her father mumble something, and finally felt the plastic grocery sacks weigh down her outreached hands. "Thanks."

Anna turned and walked stiffly back up the driveway, her heart rate slowing and her breathing normalizing.

"Well, hey, that is closer to the end of the driveway than you were last week," her father shouted from behind.

Anna turned and rested her hand on the tattered wrought iron arch with a sign that read: 3258 Route 31 - Shady Springs Dinosaur Park. Her fingertips burned. Her hands looked okay, maybe a bit blotchy from the experience of being over the border. She wondered how much longer it would be before she couldn't make it past this archway, or out the front door of the house.

"You're lying, but thanks anyway." Anna knew she had gone a bit further last week. She used to be able to walk with her mother to the end of the road, toward the highway.

"Your sister's coming by this afternoon," Jim called over his shoulder as he got back into the truck. "Try to be nice to her. She may be the only person willing to do your shopping when I am gone."

"Very funny," Anna said. Her connections to the town of Shady Springs, Iowa, and the rest of the world were already tenuous.

"Why don't you touch up the *T. rex* this weekend? There should be enough paint left in the garage."

"I'll ask Sheila to do it," Anna said. As much as she felt comfortable and familiar with the dinosaurs, she never liked getting too close.

Cement dinosaurs spotted the five-acre landscape of Shady Springs Dinosaur Park. Many were frozen in silent roars or stuck in eternal battles with each other or with cavemen. The wonder and awe of seeing such representations had dissipated from the American populace decades ago. The millions of years erroneously represented together in one place at one time could not compete with modern mechanical or digital prehistoric entertainment. The park was a relic of relics.

Anna liked the fictional landscape. She felt safe in the unreal world. Outside of the park, things were not so stagnant and predictable. Anna had not left her five-acre world in ten years.

She watched the truck turn around in the driveway, then drive back down the dirt road. She sighed. She had survived. Anna turned and walked up the driveway, toward the house. She was lucky this time.

When she reached the front door, she heard the sound of a car horn. Then the sound of glass and metal crushing suddenly exploded in the distance.

The caveman lay in the middle of the road, raised club in hand. His mouth was gaping into a silent, primal yell. His eyes were open and flat, the white paint amateurishly extending onto his brow ridge. His cement body was split in two, exposing a metal rod. His feet were connected to large, dirt-caked cement blocks. Sheila had never seen the support blocks of any of the statues in the park before today, although she knew all the statues were kept stable with blocks of varying depth. It looked almost as if the caveman were wearing platform shoes.

A few yards ahead, the remains of the Ford truck hissed and ticked in a bizarre mechanical death rattle. The hood of the truck pushed up to the shattered windshield, the rest of the front end straddled the trunk of the tree in a twisted metallic embrace. The driver's side door lay on the ground, where it had been dropped after being pried open by paramedics.

"Once I'm done here, I'll be calling on those Katz brothers." Officer Tom Billings shook his head. "Their pranks are getting worse and worse."

"A prank?" Sheila said. She could barely see Tom through the wet mascara that clumped on her lashes and stung her eyes. The Katz brothers were immature, even by fourteen-year-old standards, but Sheila couldn't believe they would do something this reckless.

"Mr. Yoder is being taken care of." Tom patted Sheila on the shoulder, then stared toward the clouds slowly shifting in the sky beyond the canopy of trees. "I had Officer Mason pick up your mother and bring her to the hospital. Why don't you go and check on your sister?"

"Anna…" The anger in Sheila's own voice jolted her. Their dad wouldn't have been driving on this dangerous, winding road if Anna would just grow up and get over her agoraphobia or whatever her neurosis du jour was these days. Sheila drew a deep breath to steady her voice. "I'll make sure she's okay."

Sheila turned, and was pulling open the door on her 2005 VW Golf, when she felt a hand on her shoulder.

"I'll stop over later tonight to talk with Anna and look around the park," Tom said. "If you don't mind."

"Of course not," Sheila said. "I'll see you shortly."

Sheila started her car and drove only twenty feet before coming to the sharp turn in the road where her father must have been surprised by a caveman. She couldn't believe the Katz brothers would do something so dangerous. Even if they were the worst kids she had ever known, she would never suspect they would be so foolish and violent.

Sheila turned a second corner and saw the driveway to her childhood home. She could see Anna sitting on the doorstep of the house, knees pulled into her chest and face resting on her knees. As she got closer, it was evident that her sister was crying. The gravel driveway crunched and popped loudly under the tires as she drove beneath the sign on the archway.

"Come on, Anna," Sheila said as she got out of the car. "Let's go inside."

Anna turned her face up to Sheila and asked, "What happened?"

"Dad hit a tree," Sheila answered.

"I heard a crash, and I called the police"—Anna was speaking quickly—"and Tom stopped up here to say everything would be okay, but he didn't tell me what happened. I heard a lot of sirens, so I don't think everything really was okay."

"Come on, let's go inside." Sheila reached her hand down to Anna, but Anna stood up on her own.

The sisters sat in the dark living room. It still had the same drab olive green carpet they had played Chutes and Ladders on as children. Sheila stared at the starving artist landscape oil painting that hung on the wall. It depicted a deep moss-colored forest at dawn with an unskilled texture of coarse strokes and piles of paint. Sheila didn't know what to say to her sister. They had grown apart over the years, and the frail woman on the couch next to her was barely reminiscent of the beautiful freckle-faced girl who used to laugh loudly at every corny joke their father cracked.

About an hour passed before there was a knock on the front door. Sheila pulled open the door to see Tom.

"I called your mom. They sent your dad over to the hospital in Ida Grove," Tom said. As he spoke, he looked over Sheila's shoulders as if he was trying to get a quick scan of the house. Sheila hoped he wasn't going to want to look inside. Once again, Anna hadn't been keeping the house up. There was an embarrassing stack of dirty dishes in the sink, and crumpled clothes in the corner of the bedroom. Tom sighed and said, "I wish I had better news for you…"

"I spoke with our mother just an hour ago," Sheila said quickly. "I know about Dad's condition."

"What condition?" Anna said. "You never told me you spoke to Mom."

"I talked to Mom when you were in the bathroom counting tiles," Sheila said. She turned back to Tom. "It's an odd habit she has that seems to calm her down."

"Your dad will be fine," Tom said loudly, peering over Sheila's shoulder and nodding toward Anna. "Now, if you don't mind, I need to take a look around the park."

"I don't mind, so long as I can come with you," Sheila said. "I can show you where that caveman came from."

"Is Anna okay?" Tom asked.

"She'll be fine," Sheila said quickly, then stepped off the cement front stoop and started walking down the gravel path toward the park. She turned and looked at Tom, who was still standing in front of the doorway to the house.

"Should we…" Tom said, nodding toward the front door.

"It'll be better if she doesn't come with us," Sheila answered before Tom could finish his question.

Anna watched from the kitchen window as Tom and Sheila strolled around the perimeter of the park, occasionally disappearing and reappearing as the path wound back and forth to various prehistoric scenes over the gently sloping hillside. Sheila occasionally stopped and pointed at statues. They stood a long time in front of the *T. rex*, as Tom leaned causally on the concrete monster's leg in conversation. Anna thought she could even see her sister sometimes smiling. Tom, maybe once or twice, allowed his lips to curve into a grin as well.

Anna held her breath as they stopped in the spot, on the far southern corner of the park, where the cavemen battled a *Stegosaurus*. One of the three cavemen was gone. Anna hadn't even noticed he was missing before, but now his absence was glaring. Her eyes quickly scanned the surrounding prehistoric scenes to see if the caveman had been moved, but she couldn't see the third caveman anywhere.

Anna watched, straining her eyes to see the expression on Tom's face as he felt the ground where the missing caveman had once stood. Sheila stood behind him, her hand on her hip, and apparently still talking. Anna could see Sheila's head was cocked in that way it always was when she was flirting. Sheila was so bold.

Eventually, Tom straightened up, and he turned to Sheila. With his back now at the house, he pointed to the other cavemen. Anna saw Sheila shrug. Then Tom turned and embraced one of the cavemen. The strain was evident, even from a distance, as his bent knees shook and his face grimaced. Tom let go of the statue and inspected its base. Pointing at the woods a few yards away from where they stood, he and Sheila disappeared into the forest.

The phone rang, surprising Anna.

"Hello?" she said after picking up the phone on the wall next to the kitchen table.

"Hi, sweetheart." It was Anna's mother. Her voice was a quiet whisper. "I was just calling to check in on you. Sheila said you were shaken up."

"How's Dad?" Anna felt terrible that Mom was in the hospital with Dad, who had just been in a serious car accident, and yet she was calling to check on her.

"Didn't Sheila tell you?" her mom said. "We got him here to the Ida Grove hospital. They say he is in stable condition. His arm is broken, he has about fifty stitches, and they're doing some tests to make sure he doesn't have internal bleeding. He's pretty out of it right now with the pain medication they gave him."

"So he's going to be okay, right?" Anna said.

"He'll be okay. He's very lucky to be alive," Anna's mom said. "Have the police checked on the Katz brothers yet?"

"I don't know. Nobody has told me anything. Do you think they have something to do with it?"

"Who else?" her mom said. "Those boys must've been waiting. They must've moved the caveman out into the road while you and your father were visiting."

"Why would they do that?" Anna said.

"Don't repeat this to Mrs. Katz, but between you me and the rest of Shady Springs," Mrs. Yoder said in a whisper, "those boys are disturbed. Just sick."

<u>Septophobia</u>
Fear of decay or decaying matter.

CHAPTER 2

Tom and Sheila walked the narrow path through the woods that divided the Katz property from the Yoder property and Shady Springs Dinosaur Park. As Sheila followed Tom, she tried to keep him engaged in conversation. Saying nothing just felt too awkward, and she was tired of hearing Tom tell her how sorry he was about her dad. Dad had finally seen the light about how destructive Anna was to the family. He was so close to taking action. A part of Sheila was almost glad it had happened, but she could never tell anyone that without sounding like a monster.

"That's really impressive that you are taking charge," Sheila said as she followed Tom. "I can see a natural leader in you."

"I just think having a dog on the force would be both cost-effective and useful," Tom said over his shoulder. "Plus, I love dogs. I figured he could live with me and I could train him myself."

"I can see a natural leader in you," Sheila repeated. She was barely paying attention to the words she was saying. She was more worried about watching where she stepped so she didn't land in any poison ivy. She realized she was flirting a bit with Tom, but it was the simplest way to interact with men. It required the least amount of effort and yielded the best results.

"I don't know if I'm much of a leader," Tom said, "but thanks for saying so."

Sheila knew she was predictably pretty. Full lips, small nose, large eyes, perfectly straight, shiny hair. She was the sort of woman guys notice on the street. She was beautiful and destined to grab the interest of most simple men. She wished she were an unexpected beauty—the type of woman who gets a first look, as well as a second. She always thought her sister had that beauty. Anna's smile was a little bit

15

uneven, but you didn't notice it at first. Then, that was all you noticed. Every time she smiled, you thought she was trying to tell you something, and it was intoxicating to those around her. Freckles subtly dotted her face and when you saw them, you realized she was beautiful without even a speck of makeup. Then you were hooked. Sheila knew she never was and never would be as beautiful as Anna. Some days it mattered; some days it didn't. Today, it mattered, and she wasn't sure why.

Sheila interjected as many encouraging sounds as she could without sounding disingenuous as she listened to Tom talk. She flirted with him for sport and out of habit more than anything else because, in reality, she truly didn't find him all that attractive. He had deep pores on his long nose, and even deeper crow's-feet around his eyes that made him look like he was always squinting. His fair skin was pink from the sun, and his hair was an unflattering strawberry blond. Still, he had nice blue eyes and perfect white teeth, which she could glimpse when he chose to smile. Plus, he wasn't married, for whatever that was worth, and there weren't that many eligible men in Shady Springs. If he ever responded to her flirtations, Sheila knew she'd probably just slap him and feign innocence. She expected that Tom realized this too.

As the woods thinned out, Sheila could see the Katz house and large front yard appear. They never kept their house or land in very good shape, and today the decay seemed a little worse than usual. A couple of tractor tires, dried and split with age, lay outside the shed. As they walked through the long grass in the front lawn, Sheila had to carefully step around hidden rusted tools, a few bottle rockets staked in the ground and forgotten, and countless empty beer cans.

"I can't believe this place," Sheila whispered at Tom, who was walking just two steps in front of her. "I told Anna that our house would be as bad as this if it wasn't for Dad and I coming over regularly."

It hit Sheila unexpectedly, but when she said 'Dad,' she felt a sudden pang of sadness. She wanted to be at the hospital with him, but her mom insisted she stay with Anna. As always, Anna's needs dictated the actions of the entire family.

"Yes, this house could be quite lovely if they would take better care of it," Tom said over his shoulder. "A big two-story home with gingerbread details and lots of land could be nice."

"Gingerbread details on a house like this look more disconcerting than whimsical," Sheila said. "Dad always hated this place."

The white paint was peeling, nearly stripped away completely in many spots. The large front porch was a cluttered storage area for bikes, toys the kids had long since outgrown, gardening tools, and old furniture. The house seemed very still. Maybe nobody was at home.

The screen door was off the hinges, and leaned up against the house, next to the front door. Tom knocked as Sheila waited at the bottom of the porch steps.

After several moments of silence, footsteps could be heard and the front door was opened by Mrs. Katz.

"Afternoon, Tom," Mrs. Katz said with more friendliness and familiarity than Sheila expected.

"Good afternoon," Tom said. He stepped back, allowing Mrs. Katz to walk out on the porch. Although it was possible that she was only ten years older than Sheila, Mrs. Katz looked like she was from another generation. Her shoulder-length hair had the last remnants of a perm, and the orange tinge of a bad bleach job.

"Hi, Sheila." Mrs. Katz seemed to not notice Sheila until she stepped onto the porch.

"How are you, Mrs. Katz?" Sheila asked.

"Probably not so good now that Tom is here," Mrs. Katz said, and a short, hoarse laugh punctuated her sentence. "What did the boys do now?"

"Well, that's what I'm hoping to find out," Tom said. "Are they home?"

"No, you just missed them," Mrs. Katz said. "They went hunting out in King's Grove. Probably won't be home until late."

"Do you know where they were this morning?" Tom asked.

"At home, I believe."

"You believe?"

"I had a late night last night." Mrs. Katz's eyes shifted to Sheila, and she looked her up and down before returning her gaze to Tom. "I only woke up about an hour ago."

Sheila felt her cheeks grow warm with the unexpected once-over. Mrs. Katz must have assumed that Sheila was going to pass judgment on the Katz family. Judgment had already been passed years ago. There were no new revelations here. Everyone in town knew Mrs. Katz was a drunk and that her sons bordered on evil.

"My father is in the hospital," Sheila said. "There was an accident this morning down on Park Road."

"I'm sorry to hear that," Mrs. Katz said. "I hope it isn't too serious."

"It is," Sheila said.

"He will be okay, but the accident was quite serious," Tom said, placing himself in the sight line between the two women.

"I'm sorry," Mrs. Katz said again. Sheila tried to peer around Tom to see the expression on her face when she said this. Her voice sounded as if she were smiling. "What does his car accident have to do with me?"

"I will need to speak with Jeremy and Matt when they get back," Tom said. "I'll stop by this evening."

"I hope you aren't implying they had anything to do with the accident. My boys are good boys," Sheila could hear Mrs. Katz say, though she still couldn't see her face. She could only see Tom's back, which crowded the doorway. "I don't understand what you are accusing them of. And why is *she* here?"

Tom turned around to Sheila and said, "Thanks for the tour of the park, but I'll need to excuse myself from your company."

Sheila struggled not to roll her eyes. Tom sounded so artificial when he tried to speak formally.

"I excuse you from my company," Sheila said. She wanted to curtsy sarcastically when she said this, but decided against it. Instead, she just nodded at Tom. Tom nodded in reply, turned, and walked into the Katz home. Mrs. Katz stared at Sheila as the door shut loudly behind him.

<u>Autophobia</u>
Fear of being alone or solitude.

CHAPTER 3

Anna was known as SuicideSue to most of her acquaintances outside of the Yoder family. All of these acquaintances existed only on the Internet and disappeared from her life as soon as her computer was turned off.

Today was a terrible day, Anna typed. *My dad is in the hospital, and I know Sheila thinks it's all my fault.* Anna sent the message. She stared at her shaking fingers until she heard a small *ding,* the voice of her anonymous friends.

<<Hugs>> It will be OK. Why would it be your fault? the message read on her computer screen.

Because Dad wouldn't be coming out here if it weren't for me. Anna sent the message. She waited for a response for what seemed liked several minutes. Nothing. Then she typed, *I can just tell that Sheila hates me.*

Sheila doesn't hate you. She hates your disease, was the response from KTMaa.

Anna was so sick of the patent drivel of support groups. People always said stuff like this, and it held no meaning.

Stop the cut-and-paste therapy. I am my disease. She hates ME, Anna wrote back. She usually wasn't so bold, but she was looking for real support today from the Agoraphobics Support Circle, and KTMaa was copying brochure-style answers.

You are not your disease, SuicideSue. You shouldn't define yourself that way, KTMaa wrote back.

Anna went to log off the session, when a new name appeared in the member's box—CrazyCorn90. She waited a few seconds to see if CrazyCorn90 would have anything to add.

This isn't a disease, was CrazyCorn90's contribution. The sentence hung on the screen silently. No one was responding to it.

Anna could feel her cheeks flush a bit. She didn't want to argue with the new member, but she was feeling bold and needy.

Explain, Anna typed slowly after some consideration.

This is a way of life, CrazyCorn90 responded.

It was the sort of sentiment that Anna was familiar with from eating disorder chat rooms, but it was the first time she had seen it stated in a support group for agoraphobics.

I have to go, Anna typed, and logged off.

Sheila couldn't stop thinking about yesterday's encounter with Mrs. Katz as she drove from her apartment in town to her childhood home at Shady Springs Dinosaur Park. As she drove past the intersection of Park Street and Forest Hill Road, she had to force herself to not turn up the road and visit the Katz family. Sheila and Mrs. Katz shared nothing in common other than a zip code, and Sheila was sure that Mrs. Katz liked it that way too.

Sheila grabbed the plastic sack of apples as she got out of her car in front of the house. She could see Anna peering out the kitchen window as she approached the front door.

"Hi," Anna said as she pulled the front door open.

"Hi, yourself," Sheila said, walking past Anna and toward the kitchen.

"Are those from Mom and Dad's tree?" Anna asked, following Sheila.

"Yes. I told Mom you'd never eat them."

"They have worms." Anna slumped into the kitchen chair.

"Yeah, I know," Sheila said. One apple, five years ago, did have a worm. But like most apples from Mom and Dad's tree, these were beautiful—clean as apples you would buy in a store, just without the waxy finish. "These apples can rot here or rot at Mom and Dad's house. At least if the apples are here, they'll think you're eating right."

"I am eating, Sheila," Anna said. "I have to go."

"Go where?" Sheila folded her arms.

"I'm supposed to meet someone online." Anna stood up.

"You don't meet people online, Anna," Sheila said. "You meet characters. You meet the artificial persona that people wish they had in real life."

"You don't know anything. You barely even use e-mail."

"If you want to meet someone, why don't you come to work with me? A lot of interesting people hang out at the bookstore."

"Thanks for the wormy apples," Anna said and walked out of the kitchen, toward her bedroom.

"You don't really know anyone online, Anna. Don't trust someone just because they have a clever screen name," Sheila called after her sister.

As Sheila walked out the front door and toward her car, she saw something was stuck under her windshield wiper. A piece of paper. She quickly scanned the driveway, then park, then gazed down the road. No one was in sight.

Sheila lifted the wiper and found the paper was tightly wrapped twice around the blade. It was a torn piece of lined paper, the ends frayed from being ripped from a spiral-bound notebook.

The handwriting was uneven, the sentences drifting above and below the lines of the paper. The letters were all uppercase, as if the writer were shouting. It read, *My boys aren't the cause of all your problems or all the problems of this town. Before you start accusing my family, maybe you should take a look at your own family. Watch your back. Sometimes very bad things come in meek and pretty little packages.*

Sheila walked back to the house and through the front door. She could hear the soft clicks of a keyboard coming from her sister's room just down the hallway.

"I'm staying with you tonight, Anna," Sheila called and folded the note into her pocket.

Ligyrophobia
Fear of loud noises.

CHAPTER 4

"Who's there?" Anna sat up in bed. Her bedroom was black, except for the sliver of light glowing under the closed door. She wasn't sure if she had heard something or if it was just part of a dream. Remembering that Sheila was staying the night, Anna relaxed a bit and lay back.

Then she heard it again, a low rumble that was somehow both earthy and unnatural. The sound surrounded her. It was so loud she was sure she felt her bed vibrate a little beneath her. Then there was silence. The sound replayed in Anna's head, allowing her to analyze what she had just heard. She thought the sound was more of a growl than a rumble. Anna closed her eyes tightly, so tightly that white stars appeared, shimmering and reassuring.

As a few moments passed, Anna once again wondered if she had dreamt that garbled low growl. It was hard to say. When pulled out of sleep at three thirty in the morning, it was difficult to decipher the real world from the unreal.

The house was still. Anna opened her eyes, staring at the sliver of light under the door. What if Anna and Sheila were not alone in the house? She imagined what she would do if a shadow suddenly eclipsed that light. Would she scream? Would she hide? Or would she just freeze up and accept her fate? The prospect of something being in the house, something that could have produced such a sound, frightened Anna more than actually seeing something. Anna knew her imagination sometimes took over every other sense in her body, including any remaining rationality.

The sliver of light continued to glow underneath the door, steady and without shadow. The house remained silent. The sound she had heard continued to replay in her mind. It couldn't have been in her imagination…could it?

Anna clenched her eyes shut once more, until she saw stars, then kicked her feet out of the cotton sheets and swung her legs out of bed. She walked blindly to her bedroom door and quickly pulled it open. Once she knew light was spilling into her bedroom, she opened her eyes. Nothing was ahead of her. Nothing was behind her. The house was so quiet that the silence was palpably pressing on her ears.

Anna walked down the hallway and to the living room, where her sister lay asleep on the couch. She must have fallen asleep while reading in her favorite spot, something she had done since she was a young girl.

"Sheila," Anna whispered. The figure on the couch did not move. Anna peered over the pile of blankets carefully to ensure that it was, indeed, Sheila who was sleeping on the couch.

Sheila's eyes opened slowly at first, and in an instant they widened as she gasped, "Anna!"

"Sorry," Anna said, and crouched next to the couch. "Did you hear something?"

"No, Anna," Sheila said and turned on her side, away from Anna. "It was just your imagination."

"Sheila"—Anna tapped her shoulder—"I am sure I heard something. It was loud, and I think my bed moved a bit."

"God," Sheila said. Then she sat up. "Let's have some tea. You'll calm down. Then we'll both go back to sleep. Okay?"

"Okay," Anna said as she helped her sister stand up.

The sisters walked into the kitchen, and Anna sat at the table as Sheila began to prepare the tea.

"Like old times, huh?" Sheila said as she pulled open the cupboard door above the stove.

Anna was surprised that her sister was being so good-natured. Maybe this was a dream too. "Yeah," Anna said. "Want to do makeovers since we are up?"

"I'm only seeing one clean mug here," Sheila said, closing the cupboard. "Why don't you clean one of the mugs by the sink?"

Anna stood and walked to the sink. She grabbed a black Iowa Hawkeye mug sitting on a kitchen towel. Just outside her peripheral vision, Anna caught a sudden movement outside the kitchen window.

"Look," Anna said, leaning over the sink and squinting out the window.

"What?" Sheila said.

Anna continued to look out the window, toward the park. The dinosaurs glowed, their paint shining in the moonlight. The treetops of the peripheral forest swayed in perfect syncopation to what must have been a warm breeze.

"Nothing," Anna said. She couldn't allow fear to overcome her in a rare moment of bonding with her sister. Anna began rinsing her mug, when once again, a movement too large to be missed caused her to look back up. Anna's eyes landed right on the largest sculpture in the dinosaur park—the *T. rex*.

At night, the *T. rex* looked like a dark cloud, strange and hanging unnaturally in the middle of a large field. The form of the *T. rex*, distinct by sheer size, was outlined by the silver of twilight. Anna squinted at the large, dark form, leaning over the sink until her nose hit the warm window glass.

Then, it moved.

It started with a small, but distinct quiver. Then the dark cloud lurched forward at least a foot. Anna heard the sound again, but wasn't sure if it was just a replay in her mind or if it was real. She felt the floor move a bit, but it might have just been her own feet shaking. She saw her sister's arms come around her from behind and squeeze her tightly. She heard her sister saying, "Stop it, Anna. There's nothing out there. Look, there's nothing…"

But the rest of her sister's words disappeared. She couldn't hear them over her own scream.

Despite the fact she was sure she had not fallen asleep all night, Anna woke up. Sunlight illuminated the small living room through a narrow window next to the entryway door.

"Sheila?" Anna said as she sat up on the couch. Her back and shoulders ached with the tension of the previous night.

"In here."

Sheila's voice came from the kitchen. The kitchen. That was where she had seen the impossible source of that sound last night.

"Sheila," Anna said again.

The sound she heard last night was organic and unnatural-sounding all at the same time, like the sound of a volcano erupting in short bursts.

"Sheila," Anna said again.

It was like the sound of a gigantic *T. rex* lurching forward on cement limbs.

"What?" Sheila appeared in the entryway that connected the living room and the kitchen. She held a small trash bag in her hand. "You're okay. See? The sun is up. Everything is fine."

"Okay." Anna looked at her sister, but had to quickly look away, as her face showed more exasperation than sympathy. She couldn't stand that look. Anna stared at the landscape painting that hung on the wall across from the couch. It was Dad's favorite painting. She looked back at her sister, whose face had softened as if she knew Anna was thinking about her father. "Hey, Sheila, Dad's doing okay, isn't he?"

"Yes," Sheila said. She had a small smile on her face, a look of relief. "You should call him today. He's still in the hospital, but Mom thinks they'll release him soon."

"What's in the bag?"

"I'm cleaning up the mug you broke last night," Sheila said.

"I don't remember that."

"I can see why." Sheila turned and began to walk toward the kitchen. "Come and help."

Anna stood and followed her sister. As she reached the entryway, the sunlight hit her. She didn't want to look out the small window next to the front door, but she had to look. She didn't know which would be more disturbing—being crazy or being right. She could see just the tip of the *T. rex* tail. The house blocked the rest of the statue. The kitchen window would give a better view.

Anna walked quickly to the kitchen window. She ignored her sister, who asked her to sweep the floor. Leaning over the kitchen sink, she squinted at the *T. rex*. It couldn't be her imagination. It clearly was in a different location than it had been yesterday, maybe even closer than it was last night after that big lurch forward. It seemed too strange to be true. Until recently, the landscape out this window had not changed since Anna was a little girl. That was the comfort of living at Shady Springs.

"You can tell that the *T. rex* moved," Anna said. The *T. rex* had betrayed her. First the caveman, now the *T. rex*.

"It hasn't moved," Sheila said. "It is just your imagination."

"You heard that sound last night, right?"

"Anna, all I heard was you screaming."

"Did you feel the floor shake?"

"No."

"And you don't think the *T. rex* has moved?"

"No," Sheila said.

"I know it has," Anna whispered.

"Do you want me to go out and look at it?" Sheila said. She surprised Anna when she put her hand on Anna's shoulder. It seemed so kind.

"Please," Anna said. The *T. rex* was clearly, if only slightly, closer to the house. Its beady black eyes looked slightly larger, its teeth slightly sharper. "Be careful."

Anna stared out the kitchen window as her sister walked toward the giant statue. As she got further away from the house, she appeared to get smaller and the *T. rex* proportionately larger. For a moment, it seemed like Sheila was the bravest person Anna had ever known.

Sheila reached the *T. rex*, and Anna watched as she patted the thick leg and craned her neck up toward the top of the statue. After a few moments, she turned her head down and seemed to squint at the ground. Sheila glanced up toward, Anna, and Anna knew Sheila wasn't looking very carefully. She was probably just trying to get Anna to shut up. Sheila then walked to the garage, reemerging moments later carrying a couple buckets of paint. Sheila always had to make a point about everything, and now she was going to taunt Anna by fearlessly retouching the beast that scared her little sister.

Anna left the kitchen window and went to her bedroom. At least her online friends would understand, even if her own sister didn't. She turned on her computer and logged on to Agoraphobics Support Circle as SuicideSue.

I know I saw something that my sister says I couldn't possibly have seen. Does that make me crazy? Anna typed. She saw the names of a few members who were nearly always online: KTMaa, AllyBi, TomFriday, AmazingGrace1976, and DarKorners. She also saw CrazyCorn90 was logged on.

Hi, CrazyCorn90, Anna typed before anyone could respond to her first post. She and CrazyCorn90 had had a long online discussion before bed last night. He, or she, had turned out to be very understanding and kind.

Hi, Anna, CrazyCorn90 wrote back. Anna smiled. It felt good to be recognized and remembered. It made her friends feel less anonymous and more real. She wished CrazyCorn90 had shared his or her real name so she could respond with a similar level of familiarity.

That depends on what you think you saw, TomFriday wrote.

Anna wasn't sure how to answer. She paused and read a few other online conversations that were happening simultaneously. One was about AmazingGrace1976's conflicting desire for a singing career with her fear of being around people. The other conversation appeared to be about DarKorners' publishing her depressing poetry in her own depressing e-zine.

Well…what did you see, Anna? KTMaa wrote.

Last night I woke up to a terrible sound, Anna wrote slowly. She didn't know how to explain this without immediately being dismissed as a liar or as someone suffering from psychotic hallucinations.

"Anna?" It was Sheila. Anna heard the front door close. Her sister's voice called out, "I'm doing a little work outside." There was a pause. Then she could hear footsteps down the hallway, and Sheila's face peered around Anna's bedroom door. "Anna?"

"I heard you," Anna said. "That was a statement. I didn't know you wanted a response."

"Do you want to give me a hand?" Sheila opened the door further and stepped into Anna's room.

"I'm busy," Anna said.

"Online?"

"Yes."

Sheila sighed loudly before turning and walking away. Anna heard the front door close.

I saw one of the dinosaurs move, Anna typed.

Do you mean one of the statues in the park? AmazingGrace1976 was the first to respond, evidently more interested in this new conversation than her talk of her unlikely singing career.

I don't know if that means you are crazy, KTMaa wrote. *LOL. But doesn't make you sane.*

Dementophobia

Fear of insanity.

CHAPTER 5

"This was the year Dad decided to put Christmas lights on the dinosaurs," Sheila said, pointing to a picture yellowed with age and pasted into her mom's scrapbook.

"I had no idea Mom put this together, " Anna said. "Did you?"

"No. She must have thought it was a significant year if it warranted an album." Sheila couldn't believe she had found the box of old pictures when she was putting the paint back in the garage.

The garage was a testimony to the family legacy of disorganized planning. Dad, in particular, was notorious for getting great deals on things that they *may* someday need. The need for these things, of course, rarely arose. When the need did present itself, Dad would excitedly dive into the garage to look for the needed item and frequently be unable to find it in all the clutter. He would often emerge, defeated, several hours later. On occasion, though, he would emerge a hero, and these rare victories would justify even more stockpiling of what-ifs and miscellany. As a result, the giant four-car garage barely had room for a single compact car. It was filled from floor to ceiling with boxes. Several large cardboard boxes were marked "free" as if they were from a roadside giveaway. Countless baskets, pieces of sports equipment, and knickknacks still bore a price tag written with permanent marker on a strip of masking tape as evidence of their garage sale origins.

"I remember that year," Anna said, still looking intently at the image of her young-looking father dressed in a black snowmobile suit and pointing to the *Stegosaurus* glowing with sporadic little specks of glowing green Christmas lights. He looked like he was laughing. "We didn't think we were going to have a white Christmas that year."

"Yes, but on the twenty-third, we had over a foot of snow drop overnight," Sheila said. She couldn't help but smile as she remembered her dad's sudden burst of Christmas spirit.

"It was like waking up in another world," Anna said. Her ceramic mug rattled as she mindlessly stirred the long-since-dissolved Splenda into her coffee.

"I love that," Sheila said. "You go to bed with everything looking so brown and dead—and wake up on this new beautiful planet, bright and white."

"I hate that. I'd rather watch the snow come down so I know what to expect. I can see it as it happens."

"You're so weird," Sheila said. She turned the page. "Here, look at this picture." She pushed the book across the kitchen table, toward Anna.

"What, Mom and Dad doing dishes?"

"No, look out the window behind them. The *T. rex*."

Anna grabbed the photo album and walked to the window. She looked out the window and then down at the photo album and then out the window again.

"It's moved." Anna handed the photo album back to Sheila. "I'd swear my life on it."

"Anna, it hasn't moved."

"The shadows are all different. You can tell it moved."

"The shadows are different because this was taken at a different time of day," Sheila said. "How can you possibly look at this picture and say the *T. rex* has moved?"

"I don't care if you think I'm lying."

"I don't think you're lying."

"I also don't care if you think I'm crazy."

"Anna…" Sheila stopped herself from arguing further with her sister. "Tom is going to meet me here in a few minutes. We may take a walk outside or even leave the park. Are you going to be okay?"

"I'll be fine." Anna sighed. "Mom and Dad were really happy that Christmas."

"So were you," Sheila said.

"This letter doesn't represent a specific threat," Tom said as he leaned against Sheila's car.

"How specific does a threat have to be—she's telling me to watch my back," Sheila said. She was glad Tom had come over in his plain clothes rather than his uniform. It gave the appearance that he was checking in on Sheila as a friend rather than as a fulfillment of law enforcement duties. It was unlikely that Tom gave this as much thought as Sheila. "Mrs. Katz is implying that I'm in some sort of danger, and I feel that is clearly a threat."

"First, you don't know this note came from Mrs. Katz," Tom said.

"Of course it came from Mrs. Katz. It talks about her boys and her family," Sheila said. "Why are you defending her? What, are you two an item or something?"

"Excuse me?"

"I mean, not that I care," Sheila said quickly. "It just seems like you may be a bit biased. I feel this woman has made a threat to me, and you are saying it isn't a threat and that you don't even know who wrote the note?"

"There are no serious crimes here," Tom said. His neck was turning splotchy and red. Sheila didn't know if that meant he was embarrassed or angry.

"The note doesn't threaten you with danger," Tom continued. "It is *warning* you of danger."

"Warning someone you may hurt them is a threat." Sheila took the note from Tom's hands.

"Informing someone who is unaware that they are in danger of being hurt by someone else is a warning," Tom said. "Even if it is difficult to accept as a possibility."

"Who would hurt me? Anna?" Sheila said after rereading the note. "Mrs. Katz seriously thinks Anna could be a threat to me?"

"We don't know it was Mrs. Katz. But I believe that is what the author of the note was saying."

"Is the author of the note also implying that Anna had something to do with my dad's car accident?"

"That could be a stretch. But, yes, possibly."

"Impossible."

"Not impossible, although it seems improbable to me," Tom said. Sheila felt her shoulders drop a bit with this revelation.

"Anna is not capable of hurting anyone other than herself," Sheila said. She glanced up the driveway and toward the house. She didn't see Anna watching like she normally would. She must have been on her computer.

"You're probably right," Tom said. "Anna is such a lovely girl. Troubled, but lovely. I can't imagine…" His voice trailed off.

"I'm sure she wasn't involved with moving the caveman. Anna loves her dad and hates pranks," Sheila said.

"It would be pretty hard to imagine how she could move that caveman statue anyway. I could barely move it myself."

"I think you are probably a little bit stronger than Anna."

"I hope so," Tom said, smiling. Then his face quickly became serious once again. "Do you know if your dad keeps a dolly of some kind in the garage?"

"I don't know," Sheila said. She glanced up the driveway, toward the garage.

"Like I said, it seems improbable that Anna would have moved the caveman. But a dolly may make it pretty easy to move," Tom said, his eyes squinting in the direction of the garage. "Once the statue was uprooted, anyway."

"You're welcome to search the garage," Sheila said. "But there is no way Anna would have had time to move the caveman. She was talking to my dad the entire time he was on the property."

"I may check out the garage later," Tom said. Then he shook his head. "I just don't know."

"What should I do about the note?"

"If you are worried about staying neighborly with Mrs. Katz, why don't you extend an olive branch?" Tom nodded down the road toward where the Katz house was hidden behind trees.

"Maybe."

"Make some pumpkin bars or something."

"Pumpkin bars?" Sheila said. "That's your advice?"

"I don't know," Tom said with a laugh. "Do whatever you ladies usually do to make nice."

"We'll see. One more thing," Sheila said. "Did you hear anything last night, by chance? Any strange weather or something?"

"No, clear night as far as I know. Of course, I went to bed pretty early. Why? What did you hear?"

"Nothing," Sheila said. She sighed, audibly enough to hopefully cause concern from Tom. But he was already standing up straight and pulling his car keys out of his pocket. "Thanks for coming over, Tom. I guess I'd better go check on Anna."

Sheila watched Tom back out of the long driveway, his pale, muscular arm bracing the passenger's seat as he looked behind his car. Sheila gave a small wave, even though she knew Tom couldn't see her, turned, and began walking up the driveway, toward the house.

Just as the sound of gravel crunching and spitting out from under the tires of Tom's car began to fade, the sound of another car approaching became louder. Sheila turned to see a small powder-blue convertible turn the corner to the driveway. She smiled at the occupants and raised her hand in acknowledgement.

The car pulled up further. It was a new T-Bird convertible. Inside were two college-age boys she didn't recognize. The blond-haired driver stopped the car and stepped out.

"Is this Shady Springs?" the blond driver asked, looking down at a cell phone in his hands.

"Yep," Sheila said as she pointed at the archway sign that was only five feet in front of the boys.

"Are you guys open?" he asked. He held up his phone. "I found you on a Web site about—"

"You can have a look around. We close at sundown," Sheila interrupted. They really no longer had official park hours. Every other month or so, retro-fanatics or college kids on a road trip would "discover" Shady Springs and make pilgrimage.

"Is this free, er…" the passenger asked as he got out of the car.

Clearly, these rich kids could afford a contribution, and Sheila quickly debated charging them twenty bucks admission.

"It's free." Sheila turned once again and walked into the house.

I can't adequately describe the sound, Anna typed quickly. *It was unreal. It was big and deep.*

Are you sure you weren't dreaming? AmazingGrace1976 replied.

How could you tell it moved if it was dark out? TomFriday asked.

Anna normally took a long time to respond to posts. She would make sure everything was spelled right and that she was saying everything exactly as she meant to say it. But right now her fingers were barely under her own control. They slipped from key to key with dexterity Anna didn't know she had, trying to keep up with the manic dialogue in her head, trying to justify what she saw, or what she thought she saw.

I know I wasn't dreaming because my sister was awake and saw everything. Everything except for what I saw, anyway. Anna surprised herself that she didn't edit what she wrote or even bother to read it before posting it. *And the moonlight last night was more than enough light to see the…*

"Did you hear me?" the bedroom door opened just wide enough for Sheila's head to pop through. "Christ, Anna, you're still online. How many screens do you have open? You're crazy."

"Yes?" Anna quickly posted her last message even though she hadn't finished her sentence. "What do you want?"

"I just wanted to tell you," Sheila said, fully opening the door, "there are a couple of cute guys here checking out the park."

"I don't care," Anna said. She turned back to look at the message screen.

Maybe you need to increase your meds! LOL! AmazingGrace1976 wrote.

Sorry you are going through a tough time. *hug* CuddleBear95 posted.

<this space intentionally left blank> was TomFriday's response.

What if it's a poltergeist? JamieMatthews wrote. *(Just kidding, btw.)*

"Are you still here?" Anna said, her eyes not looking away from the computer screen.

"No, I have things to do. A life to get on with," Sheila muttered, and Anna heard the door close.

What do you mean a poltergeist? Anna typed. For the first time since logging in to this session, it seemed as if several minutes passed before a response was posted. Everything slowed down. Even Anna's thoughts began to slow down as her mind fixated on the word "poltergeist."

You know, a supernatural force. CrazyCorn90's response appeared after the startling *ding.*

Anna wrote the word "poltergeist" several times on the pad of paper next to her keyboard. The computer continued to ding with more responses, but Anna stared at the word. It was the only thing that made sense at that moment, and that brought her calm.

Anna closed out the session on the Agoraphobics Support Circle without even reading the other responses. A small part of her was surprised at her own abrupt behavior and hoped the other members wouldn't hate her for logging off without saying good-bye.

Anna pulled up a search engine on her browser and typed in "poltergeist." There were 3,190,532 matches.

"Wow. She lives," Sheila said flatly as Anna walked into the kitchen. Anna wasn't sure how much time had passed, but it was still light outside.

"Shut up," Anna said, but she intentionally did not smile when she said this as she normally did. "What are you doing?"

"I'm making apple bars for Mrs. Katz," Sheila said. She was standing over the sink, peeling apples.

"Wormy apple bars?"

"Yeah." Sheila laughed. "Nothing but the best for our good neighbor."

"May I ask why?"

"I'm just trying to make nice with her. I did bring the police to her doorstep and basically accused her boys of putting Dad in the hospital."

"So, you don't think the boys are responsible?" Anna said, although she knew the boys couldn't be blamed for a restless spirit.

"I don't know who is responsible," Sheila said without looking away from her rapid-fire apple peeling. "But we are stuck with them as neighbors, so we can at least try to keep things as friendly as possible."

"Right," Anna said, although unconvinced. Sheila had never had an interest in being friendly to the Katz family before. She must have known for a fact that those boys were wrongly accused. Maybe she had seen the *T. rex* move the other night. Maybe she knew there was something else happening here. Anna could feel a small, tingling panic raise the hairs on her arms. "I'll be right back."

Anna left her sister in the kitchen and walked out the front door. The warm air hit her immediately, and she took in a suffocating breath. It was a miserably hot day. Anna turned and looked at the kitchen widow. Sheila was looking out at her, but looked back down as soon as they made eye contact. Anna thought Sheila looked just like their mother in that moment, and instantly decided *not* to tell her that later.

It didn't look like the "cute boys" were still around. Maybe her sister had made that up just get Anna to come outside. As her eyes scanned the park, she definitely felt like she was alone. She was as alone as one could be surrounded by statues staring back at you with black, vacant eyes.

She walked stiffly toward the *T. rex*. She didn't look around. She just stared at the ground ahead of her. Now that she had left the safe parameters of the sidewalk outside the house, she had to commit to moving forward. If she looked up and she saw something she didn't want to see, she'd get scared and run back to the house. Instead, she focused on placing one foot forward, and then the next. She felt the warm breeze wrapping heat around her body in a suffocating embrace. Her temperature comfort zone was probably only ten degrees wide. She had become more sensitive to heat and cold in the last few years. She had become more sensitive to everything.

With one final step, she was staring at the wide, misshaped feet of the concrete dinosaur. Her neck was locked down, and she didn't even know what she was looking for—but she was looking for it intently. A sign of movement, evidence of tampering, anything to confirm that what she had seen was real.

The *T. rex* had three toes extending out from each triangular foot. A four-inch hook-shaped claw extended out of each toe. It was clear the sculptor, Anna's grandfather, had taken more time making the claws just right than any other part of the foot. Anna's grandfather had started the park in the 1950s, in the height of dinosaur park popularity. His designs had never been updated or changed. Just a fresh coat of paint every other year and periodic touch-ups as needed. The layers of paint slightly added to the deformity of the statues.

It didn't look like the *T. rex* had moved since her grandfather first placed him there. Anna placed the palm of her hand on the hot cement leg and pushed. The *T. rex* was solid. Now with both hands, Anna pushed against the *T. rex*, grunting with effort. Nothing. Anna sighed and looked back at the house, where she could see Sheila staring out the kitchen window.

<u>Megalophobia</u>
Fear of large objects.

CHAPTER 6

The unmistakable sound woke Anna up. She reached down and quickly turned on the lamp she had placed next to her bed before falling asleep. For several moments, all Anna could hear was her own heart pulsing as she held her breath and listened.

The unearthly sound, real and unreal all at once, filled her ears. The bed shook slightly. Anna instinctively covered her ears—which muted the sound for less than a second before it stopped.

It couldn't be in my head, Anna thought. *If it were, the sound wouldn't mute when I plugged my ears.*

Without allowing herself to fully think about what she was about to do, Anna swung her feet out of bed. The faster she moved, the better.

As Anna ran, her bare feet quickly became cold in the damp grass. *But then, the mind is a very powerful thing,* Anna thought. *It can create sophisticated illusions that even fool itself. Maybe the sound seemed muted when I covered my ears because I expected it to sound muted.*

Her eyes fixed forward on the feet of the *T. rex*. *I have to know if that sound was real or if I'm crazy. I have to know if the T. rex is moving.*

She could sense movement in the corners of her eyes, but she refused to turn and look. She knew if she saw someone out here, or if she saw one of the statues moving while she was out here, she would start to scream and never stop. She couldn't let that happen, not before she got to the *T. rex*. She had to see the *T. rex*. She had to know. Too much about her sanity and her understanding of the world rested on knowing what was happening.

She moved quietly, but the sound of her toes sweeping through the grass was deafening. If Sheila woke up and saw

45

her out here, she would tell Mom, Dad, Mrs. Katz, Tom, and everyone else that Anna was crazy. Maybe she would even think Anna was out here to secretly move the statues herself. She'd say that Anna had created all this drama, and maybe crazy Anna had even fallen for her own hoax.

Details on the thick leg of the *T. rex* became visible as Anna neared. She could see the painted scales mixed with the bumpy imperfections of the cement. It looked like the trunk of a strange palm tree, thick and foreign-looking.

At first, it seemed as if light was hitting the grass next to the *T. rex* leg in a very strange way. As Anna stepped right next to the cement dinosaur, it became clear that there was a band of grass that was lighter in color, approximately one inch in width, along the side of the foot. It was dead grass. Anna leaned over. She could feel her entire body tremble as she examined the ground.

The band of dead light brown blades of grass had the same shape as the *T. rex*'s clawed foot. At least two more inches of dirt separated the band of dead grass and the dinosaur's foot. The dirt was packed hard under the weight of the giant cement creature and had not been exposed in well over half a century.

Nausea and dizziness swept over Anna in an instant. The unreal was real. The dinosaur *had* moved. And now she was in the middle of the park, and these concrete monsters were somehow alive.

It was the sound of a scream that woke Sheila up at approximately two thirty in the morning. She had been sleeping in her own old bedroom, which was now a guest room. Her hand absently searched the top of her comforter for the TV remote. The scream sounded again and was followed by a strange and loud sob. It sounded as if it were coming from outside. Sheila opened her eyes. The TV wasn't on. *Anna.*

Sheila got up and ran so quickly she was running blind with tunnel vision for several seconds. She pushed open the door to Anna's bedroom. There was a lamp sitting on the floor, illuminating an empty bed. The cries continued— horrified and pathetic-sounding. It sounded like a child crying, defenseless and terrified, hoping that Mom would come save her before the bogeyman wrapped his claws tightly around her throat.

Sheila ran out of Anna's room, down the hallway, and into the living room. She saw the front door was open. *What if there is someone in the house? What if someone came in and took Anna and is doing something horrible to her?* As the cries continued, Sheila had to move forward. She quickly, but cautiously looked out the screened door. She couldn't see much of anything in the dark.

"Anna?" Sheila called out. The sobbing continued. Sheila wondered for a moment if it wasn't Anna at all. It didn't really sound like her. What if this was some weird prank perpetrated by the Katz brothers?

"Anna?" Sheila called again. The sound of the person crying, and sometimes interjecting little yelps and gasps, continued. There was no response. Sheila opened the front door and stepped out. As her bare feet hit the cool pavement, she wondered if she'd be able to outrun whoever was out here.

"I'm coming out," Sheila said. "It'll be okay." She began walking toward the sound of the cries, squinting into the darkness for any sign of movement.

"Anna?" Sheila called again. Then she saw a figure lying on the ground at the foot of the *T. rex*. "Anna? It's Sheila."

Sheila ran to her.

"Anna?" Sheila knelt next to Anna and placed her hand on her shoulder. Anna wasn't responding. She was shaking and crying. Anna felt so light and fragile as Sheila lifted her trembling body.

"It's okay, Anna," Sheila whispered.

Anna didn't sleep until the sun began to rise. Sheila stayed with her on the living room couch. She played with her hair or gently rubbed her shoulders. When she stopped making physical contact, even for a second, Anna seemed to panic. As Anna finally fell asleep, Sheila carefully slid off the couch and skillfully replaced her lap with a pillow for Anna's head.

It was only 5:35, but Sheila knew her mom would already be awake. She was only sleeping about an hour at time. Hospital staff had encouraged her to go home and rest, but she refused to leave her husband's side. Sheila tried not to think about the fact that she hadn't been allowed to go see her father, as her mother insisted that Anna not be left alone. As much as she didn't want to burden her mom with news about Anna, she knew that this type of episode was the precise reason her mom wanted her at home.

Sheila grabbed the cordless phone off the kitchen wall and quietly walked out the front door, giving one last glance at Anna sleeping on the couch before closing the door behind her.

Sheila found the stillness of the dawn to be a bit unsettling. Maybe it was her exhaustion, but something felt different outside. It had been an unnerving night. Sheila quickly dialed the phone.

"Yoders' mobile." Sheila's mom had answered her phone in the same way ever since she and Dad purchased their first cell phone. Her cheerful voice sounded unfazed by an early morning call, or by the fact that the call was being received in a hospital room.

"Hi, Mom. How's Dad?"

"Sheila, sweetheart," her mom said. "Your father is doing really well. They are going to let him go home this morning!"

"Wow," Sheila said.

"So how are you?" Mrs. Yoder said. "This is an early morning for you, isn't it?"

"No, it's a late night," Sheila said. She looked into the living room window, trying to see if Anna was still on the couch. It didn't look like she was moving.

"Everything okay?"

"Not really, Mom. Anna had a bad night. She had a terrible panic attack, and she's only now falling asleep."

"Oh no…" Sheila heard her mom's voice trail off.

"I'll stay by her today. I'll have to run to work for a couple of hours tonight, though."

"You're a good sister."

"If this happens again, we really should call Dr. Fergus," Sheila said. "Maybe he can convince her to consider medication again."

"Or hospitalization," Mrs. Yoder said.

Sheila was surprised to hear her mom suggest this. She had suggested it years ago, and even convinced her father it was a good idea to get Anna into an inpatient program. But Mom always held out, saying that the family was all Anna needed.

"Maybe," Sheila said. She didn't want to scare her mom by revealing her enthusiasm for the idea. "So when will we see you?"

"Well, your father is feeling really good. After we get released here, we will go home and rest, and then we are planning to both come out and visit you girls this afternoon. We can stay there while you run to work."

"Don't push Dad too hard," Sheila said. "But I'd love to see him, and so would Anna."

"See you this afternoon!"

"Wait, Mom," Sheila said with some hesitation. "If you do happen to see Dr. Fergus today, will you tell him to expect a call?"

"Thank you for inviting me in," Sheila said as she stepped through the doorway of the Katz house.

"How's your father?" Mrs. Katz asked.

"He's being sent home now, and doing much better," Sheila said. "Thanks."

Sheila tried not to let her eyes look around the Katz house too much. She was afraid the look of disgust on her face couldn't be concealed. It was full of boxes, old newspapers, clothes, and garbage. In a way, it reminded Sheila of their garage, but it wasn't as orderly. There was also a distinct odor of cigarette smoke, alcohol, and garbage.

"What brings you here?" Mrs. Katz folded her arms when she said this, then looked at the Tupperware in Sheila's hands.

"I brought you some bars," Sheila said. "Apple bars. Sort of a peace offering, I guess."

"I don't care much for apples," Mrs. Katz said. "But the boys might eat them."

Sheila handed Mrs. Katz the Tupperware. "Are the boys home?"

"They are," Mrs. Katz said. "They're sleeping."

Sheila nodded as if this was normal. It was two fifteen in the afternoon.

"Well, perhaps you and I could sit down and have a little talk," Sheila said. "Neighbor to neighbor."

Mrs. Katz gestured toward the living room, and Sheila walked to the sofa. Moving aside a stack of junk mail, she sat down. Mrs. Katz sat in the folding chair next to the sofa and placed the apple bars on the floor by her feet. *And that is where those apple bars will stay and rot,* Sheila thought.

"First, thanks again for inviting me in." Sheila thought her own voice sounded a bit nervous. "Second, I received a note on the windshield of my car. I was wondering if—"

"I wrote that," Mrs. Katz interrupted. She smiled a little, as if she had won a little mind game Sheila didn't realize they were playing. "Is that why you are here?"

"Well, in part, yes," Sheila said. "You see, I want to apologize. You are right that I made assumptions that your boys were involved in the prank with the caveman, when I have no evidence of that."

"Thank you," Mrs. Katz said.

Sheila saw her smile curl a bit more in the corner of her mouth. This time, she couldn't tell if it was smug self-satisfaction or if Mrs. Katz was attempting to appear genuine.

"Thank you for accepting my apology," Sheila said.

"How is your sister?" Mrs. Katz asked.

"She's doing okay," was all Sheila could think to say. But then, before she could stop herself, she said, "Why do you ask? Did Tom tell you there was a problem with Anna?"

"No." Mrs. Katz leaned back in the chair and folded her arms. "Why should he? I was just asking you a friendly question, neighbor to neighbor."

"Anna is doing fine," Sheila said.

"What is wrong with her anyway?"

"There's nothing wrong with her."

"I don't remember the last time I saw her in town," Mrs. Katz said. Sheila didn't respond. Mrs. Katz lowered her voice and added, "I hear that she is afraid to leave her own front yard."

"Where did you hear that?"

"Oh, come on, Sheila. That's common knowledge."

"Common knowledge? That sounds like a reliable source."

"Don't get defensive. I was simply asking what's wrong with your sister." Mrs. Katz was frowning and jutting out her lower jaw. "I can believe what I hear out there, or you can tell me the truth of what is going on with your sister."

"She has agoraphobia."

"What does that mean?" Mrs. Katz asked. She leaned forward in her chair. The creases between her eyes deepened as she looked at Sheila.

"It's complicated," Sheila said. "Technically, it's a fear of open spaces. But it is much more complicated than that."

"Sort of a fear of living, then."

"Sort of."

"Is she crazy?"

"No."

"I think she is," Mrs. Katz said. "And so does everyone else."

"Okay, then," Sheila said, standing up.

"But it doesn't mean I don't feel sorry for her," Mrs. Katz said as Sheila turned to walk toward the front door.

"Anna doesn't need your pity," Sheila said. "In fact, I feel sorry for people with nothing better to do than gossip about a person they hardly know."

"Hardly know? I've known her for her entire life."

"But you don't really know her at all. You just know stories about her from the other gossips in town."

"If I don't know her," Mrs. Katz said, "it's only because your family is too uppity to get to know our family."

"You want to talk about pity…Do you want to know who I feel sorry for?" Sheila asked.

"Not really."

"I feel sorry for people who leave unsigned notes on their neighbors' cars because they don't know how to communicate like a human being."

"Now, hold on—"

"I also feel sorry for people that haven't seen their carpet in twenty years because they've never owned a vacuum or taken a trash bag to the dump."

"You'd better leave." Mrs. Katz pointed at the door behind Sheila.

"But Anna? I have no reason to feel sorry for her," Sheila said. Then she heard footsteps coming down the stairs. She stopped. The boys were awake. Sheila froze.

"Morning, Jeremy. Morning, Matt," Mrs. Katz said to her sons, but continued to stare at Sheila. "You boys know Sheila, Mr. and Mrs. Yoder's oldest daughter."

The two young men pushed past Sheila and entered the living room. They looked taller than Sheila remembered from the last time she had seen them. They were both tall, skinny, and pale. Jeremy had a rudimentary goatee and unwashed shaggy brown hair. Matt had shaved his head since the last time Sheila had seen him. Now all that was left were little black dots peppering his white scalp.

Neither of the boys acknowledged Sheila or their mom. Jeremy shoved his hands into the couch cushions and was feeling around. Matt watched, then turned to his mom.

"We need money," he said flatly.

"What for?" Mrs. Katz said.

Sheila wondered if she should leave. Why had Tom suggested this? The visit was a complete disaster. Tom didn't know anything about Katz-Yoder politics.

"Pool," Jeremy said. He pulled his hands out of the couch, apparently unsuccessful in his search.

"I don't have any money," Mrs. Katz said.

Jeremy left the living room and walked into the dining room next door. After he disappeared around the corner, the sound of shuffling and the clanging of keys could be heard.

"Hey!" Mrs. Katz yelled and started toward the dining room.

Jeremy reappeared in the doorway, clutching a few dollar bills in his hands. "You had money," he said as he walked past his mom and toward the front door. Matt followed him, shrugging at his mom as if he had no excuse for his brother's behavior.

The two boys walked by Sheila on the way out the front door. Her stomach tightened as Jeremy brushed past her, then stopped.

Jeremy turned and whispered at Sheila, "Watch out for the *Stegosaurus*."

The boys cackled in unison as they ran down the front steps.

"Don't mind them," Mrs. Katz said. She sounded surprisingly apologetic. "You know boys at that age."

"Yeah," Sheila said, although she didn't know any other boys their age. She had a coworker with a son a couple years younger but with twice the maturity. "Mrs. Katz, I'm sorry I lost my temper a bit. I guess I just get a little protective of Anna."

"Maybe that's part of the problem," Mrs. Katz said. She raised her eyebrows in a way that was exceptionally annoying to Sheila, as if she had said something really insightful and thought-provoking.

"Have a good afternoon," Sheila said as she walked through the still-open front door.

"You do the same," Mrs. Katz said.

Just as Sheila thought they had maybe ended things on a positive note, she heard the door slam behind her. "Enjoy your wormy apple bars," she muttered as she walked back toward Shady Springs Dinosaur Park.

<u>Iatrophobia</u>
Fear of doctors.

CHAPTER 7

"Anna, you look pale." Mrs. Yoder touched Anna's face. Her fingertips felt warm and soft, just like they did twenty years ago when Anna was still a little girl.

"I'm fine," Anna said.

"Are you eating?"

"I'm eating," Anna said. It was her least favorite question. Now she had to worry that her mom would get up from the kitchen table and start to look through her cupboards. Then she'd see that the same food was sitting there and rotting that had been sitting up there the last time she checked.

"A mother has to ask," Mrs. Yoder said. She looked at Anna with an uncertain expression on her face. Anna absentmindedly stirred the tea around in her mug, the spoon loudly clanging on the side of the ceramic cup. "You need to take better care of yourself."

"Is Dad going to be okay?" Anna asked quickly, almost cutting her mother off.

"Yes," Mrs. Yoder said. She smiled and leaned back in the kitchen chair, looking toward the living room. She lowered her voice to a whisper. "This is his first day out of the hospital, and he's still on pain meds. He's just a little tired."

"He can sleep in a bed. He doesn't have to sleep on the couch," Anna said.

"That's okay, dear," Mrs. Yoder said. "It's only four thirty, and he never let himself go to bed this early."

"But he's sleeping. He can't be that comfortable with his cast."

"But the couch is just a nap. The bed would mean 'going to bed.'"

"What?" Anna said, shaking her head.

"Just let him stay on the couch, and don't try to dissect the psychology of your father."

"All right." Anna stood up and walked to the kitchen window. Her eyes fell immediately on the *T. rex*. She could see the line of dead grass and dirt near its feet. She forced herself to pause before reacting. The more she stared at the line of dead grass, the more she was unsure that she was even seeing it. It could be there, or her mind could be drawing dead grass in for her so she could justify the last twenty hours of fear she had suffered.

"Anna"—her mom was next to her now—"Sheila told me you've been feeling troubled lately."

"Troubled? I'm sure that's the word Sheila used."

"Are you upset about your father? Because he is going to be just fine, I promise."

"No," Anna said. "I mean, of course I'm upset about him. But…that's not it."

"What is it, then?" Anna's mom put her hand on Anna's shoulder.

Anna thought for a moment about telling her. She looked at her mom, then back at the *T. rex*. "Nothing. I'm fine."

"Anna, if you can't talk to me—who will you talk to?"

"I don't need to talk to anyone. There's nothing to talk about," Anna said, but her eyes couldn't get off the *T. rex* and that strip of dead grass and dirt. Why didn't anyone else see it? "And, besides, I'm fine."

"I saw Dr. Fergus today," Mrs. Yoder said.

"Mom." Anna turned to her mother. She could feel herself begin to shake a bit in anger. "I am not crazy. I am not going to talk to Dr. Fergus."

"I didn't say you have to."

"He's creepy and kind of a quack."

"Okay, then. No Dr. Fergus…" Something in her mom's face changed at that moment. Sadness seemed to sweep over all of her features at once. "Because you're fine."

Anna walked past her mom and to her bedroom. Her dad was still asleep on the couch, and snoring loudly, as she passed the living room. She closed her bedroom door behind her.

Anna sat down at her computer and logged on to the Agoraphobics Support Circle. TomFriday, CrazyCorn90, and AmazingGrace1976 were in a discussion.

We shouldn't laugh…It could happen to any of us, AmazingGrace1976 wrote.

No. Saying that implies that we are all insane, CrazyCorn90 wrote.

The power of the mind is terrifying, TomFriday wrote.

There was a pause. No new text appeared.

Hi, everyone, Anna finally wrote.

Hi, Anna, AmazingGrace1976 wrote.

Anna felt a little lift, as she was surprised by the name recognition.

How are you? CrazyCorn90 wrote.

OK. Anna typed slowly. *I had a tough night, and now my parents are here.*

I'm glad you have support, AmazingGrace1976 wrote.

Anna frowned. *They aren't really that helpful,* she typed, and felt guilty before she sent the message. She deleted the line and rewrote, *Yes, they try to be supportive.*

There were no responses. Anna sighed. She could either go out and face her mother or waste a bit more time here.

What's the big topic tonight? Anna wrote. *I feel like I walked into the middle of a lively discussion.*

We were just talking about someone who completely lost her mind, Tom Friday wrote after a pause.

Almost instantaneously, a message from CrazyCorn90 was posted. It read: *You, Anna.*

Anna suddenly felt dizzy. *Ha ha, very funny,* she wrote, her fingers shaking as she typed, causing her to miss a keystroke. *Whatevew.*

Seemingly all at once, the message board was empty. CrazyCorn90, AmazingGrace1976, and TomFriday all logged off.

You guys weren't talking about me, Anna typed. *I'm not crazy.*

Mythophobia
Fear of myths, lies, or false statements.

CHAPTER 8

"I'm only here for three hours," Sheila said as the front door to Dog Day Books chimed with her arrival.

"That's fine," Barbara Swanson said. She barely looked up at Sheila and seemed to be trying to enter something into the computer by the cash register. The small bookstore had no customers, and the rows of books were completely orderly.

"What are you working on?" Sheila said. She put her purse down behind the register kiosk. At least Mrs. Swanson didn't seem to care about Sheila's sporadic hours. It was probably for the best, since it had been a slow month and the Swansons may not have enough to pay Sheila for any overtime.

"I got an e-mail from Book-It," Barbara said. She was squinting at the computer. "You know, the Web site that is sort of a clearinghouse for local book stores to fulfill local orders?"

"Yes," Sheila said. "Did we get an order?"

"I guess so. I just hate these order forms they send to us. They are always so confusing." Barbara sighed and looked over at Sheila. "Good lord, Sheila. You look terrible."

"Sorry."

"You poor thing, how could I forget?" Barbara said, standing up and turning to Sheila. "I heard about your father. Is he doing better?"

"He's doing much better."

"Is that why you can't stay? You need to go help take care of him?"

"Yeah, family stuff," Sheila said.

The door chimed, startling Sheila.

"Good afternoon," Sheila began saying before she even looked to see who had walked through the front door. It was Tom.

"Good afternoon, ladies," Tom said.

"Harold hates it when you park your car like that," Barbara said with a small laugh.

Sheila looked out the long glass panes that created the storefront of Dog Day Books. She could see Tom's cruiser parked at an angle, covering two parking spots directly in front of the store.

"Well, I can see Harold isn't working today," Tom said. "But don't worry. I'm not staying long."

"Is everything okay?" Sheila asked.

"Just fine," Tom said. "Sheila, I just wanted to let you know that I spoke with the Katz brothers."

"And they say they didn't do it, right?"

"Right."

"Do you believe them?" Sheila asked. She could see Barbara turn back to the computer, but she knew that she was listening to every word with great interest. Barbara had a bad habit of tilting her head whenever she was listening carefully to something. Her head was tilted right now.

"I don't want to condemn them just because they have a bad reputation," Tom said. "I really don't have any evidence that they were responsible."

"Great," Sheila sighed.

"Don't worry, this investigation isn't closed yet," Tom said. "I'll keep riding those boys, and eventually they'll crack. At least, I bet Jeremy will crack. He'll brag to someone about it, and it will eventually get back to me."

"Did you just get back from talking to Matt and Jeremy?" Sheila asked.

"Yes, why?"

"Where are they?"

"They're playing pool at the rec center," Tom said. "But I'd just stay away from them. You won't get anywhere talking with those two."

"You might be right," Sheila said. "You know, I took your advice and brought some apple bars to Mrs. Katz."

"Good for you," Tom said. "I'm glad that at least someone listens to my advice."

"I think I made matters worse."

"Oh," Tom said and coughed. He looked genuinely disappointed. "Sorry."

After Tom left, Sheila and Barbara were both silent for a moment. Finally, Barbara turned to Sheila and said, "The Book-It order is for your sister."

"Really?" Sheila said. She could feel her cheeks flush a bit and suddenly felt very hostile toward her sister. "That's nice. She must be using Mom and Dad's credit card to do some shopping online."

"How is Anna?" Barbara asked. Her eyes were wide when she said this, as if she were anticipating a tragic answer to her question.

"She's fine," Sheila said. "What book did she order?"

Barbara looked uneasy as she pointed at the screen. Sheila leaned over and read the title on the order. "*Understanding Metaphysics*. She's so weird."

"She isn't into that sort of thing," Barbara said slowly. "Is she?"

"Metaphysics?" Sheila asked. "Not that I know of. But she gets into weird little obsessions and interests sometimes. Usually she just reads about it online. She must be really curious to have purchased a book."

Barbara shook her head. "I don't understand how a good Christian girl raised in Shady Springs could have any interest in metaphysics. Harold put that book in stock because he thought preteen boys would like it. Something about Harry Potter."

Sheila tried to not laugh.

Three hours passed with only four customers coming by and only one of those customers purchasing a book. It was Lillian, a middle-aged kindergarten teacher who typically shopped at the bookstore once a week for romance novels.

S. A. Nicola

Today she bought three new bodice rippers. When she left the store, the books were wrapped up tightly in a brown grocery bag and tucked under her arm like a secret vice. Romance readers were always the best repeat customers.

The rec center parking lot was mostly empty, with only three cars parked by the front entrance. The building probably looked crisp and modern in the 1970s, but now the single-story building made of brick and bright orange glass looked like a dilapidated time traveller. A sign over the main entrance read: Recreation Center of Shady Springs.

Sheila parked her VW and yanked up the parking brake. She stared at the building for several minutes before deciding to get out of the car.

When she walked in the front door, the smell of stale cigarette smoke greeted her. Candy and soda machines lined the corridor. The indoor basketball court was through the door to the right, and to the left were four pool tables. Two older men Sheila recognized, but didn't know by name, were playing pool at the table closest to the door. The taller of the two men, with a red mustache, nodded and smiled at her. She nodded back, as if they shared some sort of secret understanding and hoped that would be the end of their interaction. She felt conspicuously out of place.

Sheila walked down the corridor, trying to make her appearance at the rec center seem purposeful. She imagined she might even just walk to the rear exit, then walk around the building and back to her car. She just felt too foolish to simply turn around and walk out because the Katz brothers were no longer here playing pool.

As Sheila neared the door to the basketball court, she could hear the screeching of shoes on hardwood floors. She looked in the door and saw Matt Katz chasing Jeremy Katz in a large circle in the center of the court as Jeremy held a

64

red rubber kickball to his chest. The boys looked like lanky white skeletons, with large heads, chasing each other.

Matt was the first to stop and stare in Sheila's direction. Moments later, Jeremy stopped running too. He looked back at Matt. Sheila heard one of them mumble something. Jeremy dropped the ball he was holding, and it bounced loudly, the sound echoing in the empty court. Sheila tried to smile. She had to look casual; she couldn't be intimidated by what were essentially children.

"Hi, guys," Sheila said with what she knew was a forced tone in her voice. The boys looked at each other again and then back at Sheila. "Mind if I talk to you for a minute?"

"No," Matt said. He ran his hand over his shaved head.

Sheila waited for a minute, hoping Matt and Jeremy would come meet her by the door. Instead, they just stared at her. Jeremy began to snicker, until Matt mumbled something that immediately silenced his brother.

Sheila stepped into the basketball court. The hard heels of her shoes clapped loudly with every step, the sound echoing in the large, empty room. The boys didn't move. They simply eyed her up and down and occasionally glanced at each other.

"I need to talk to you about what happened with my father," Sheila said.

Matt's shoulders fell a bit, almost as if he was relieved. "Oh, the caveman thing." He smiled a bit. "I thought we were in trouble about something."

"You might be in trouble about this," Sheila said. "You two haven't been cleared yet."

"We didn't do anything," Jeremy said. As he shook his head, his shaggy brown hair swayed and then hung down, greasy, in his face.

"Shut up, Jeremy," Matt said and then walked closer to Sheila.

"You are telling me you didn't touch that caveman?" Sheila asked.

"No, we did not," Matt said. His voice seemed to be a lower register. His eyes looked concerned and sincere. He suddenly seemed to be not just one of the notorious Katz brothers, but an honest young man. "I swear to you."

"How did that caveman get moved to the middle of the road, then?" Sheila said.

"I don't know," Matt said.

"You know there wasn't anyone else around that day except for you two, your mom, and Anna."

"I realize that, ma'am," Matt said. "I know it looks very suspicious."

"Yes, it does."

"Especially since Jeremy and I are usually picked on by Tom and everyone else in this town. People just assume if something bad happens that it's because we did it."

"Because that is usually true," Sheila said.

"That's just the thing," Matt said. "I know it is usually true. This time, though, it isn't true."

"Why should I believe you?" Sheila asked.

"Jeremy and I weren't even home when it happened. We were hunting at King's Grove. We got a dead squirrel to prove it."

"A dead squirrel doesn't prove anything. Did anyone see you at King's Grove?"

"No," Jeremy said. Matt scowled at his brother. Jeremy continued quickly. "But our mom knew we left to go hunting way before the accident happened."

"Listen," Matt said, "I don't know how to prove that we didn't do it. In fact, we don't even *have* to prove it to you. The truth will come out, I know it."

"Yeah, just ask my mom," Jeremy said. "She'll tell you we weren't home when this happened. Ask the squirrel we shot. He'll tell you where we were."

"Hell, I'd take a lie detector test if it would get you and Tom off our backs," Matt said.

"Really?" Sheila said. She studied his face, challenging him to back down.

"Absolutely," Matt said. "He's just an old man, we'd never hurt your dad. He's always been nice to us."

"I could arrange for Tom to hook up a lie detector test," Sheila said, although she had no idea if this was true. Threatening to use a test, and seeing if the boys backed down, would have to suffice.

"Yes, I *told* you I'd take the lie detector test," Matt said, sounding a little annoyed. "We didn't touch that caveman."

As Sheila walked away from the Katz brothers, she heard the screeching of shoes on hardwood begin again, and turned as she saw the boys tackling the kickball that had rolled to the sidelines.

To Sheila's surprise, she believed them.

<u>Syngenesophobia</u>
Fear of relatives.

CHAPTER 9

"Anna, I don't understand why you object so strongly to Dr. Fergus," Anna's dad said. Mr. Yoder was sitting up on the couch, sleep marks indenting his face. The cast on his forearm looked heavy, as if it were responsible for pulling his posture down into a slump.

"Why is everyone so interested in me?" Anna said. The living room felt humid. The late summer air had forced itself in through the cracks of the old house. The scrutiny only made the air feel heavier. "You're the one who was in a car accident, Dad. You're the one wearing a cast."

"Honey, you know we've been concerned about your health for some time," Mrs. Yoder said. She sat down next to Anna's father on the couch. Her brief smile to Anna looked forced and insincere.

"Stop saying 'health,' and start saying what you mean," Anna said. Her parents stared at her blankly. "You mean 'sanity.'"

"Okay." Mrs. Yoder frowned. It was uncharacteristic of Anna's mother to frown in such a pronounced manner. The lines around her mouth deepened, making her look much older and even a little bit frail. "We think that…" she began to say, and then trailed off. She shook her head and stared down at her hands folded in her lap.

"I know I cause everyone a lot of stress," Anna said. "I'm sorry. I'm sure you all resent me right now."

"We don't resent you, Anna," Anna's mother said.

"Anna"—Mr. Yoder grimaced as he leaned forward, awkwardly protecting his broken arm from movement— "don't talk like that. That's just giving unreasonable fears a voice and making them valid."

"Jeez, Dad, what self-help book have you been reading?" Anna said.

Her dad didn't even fake a laugh or smile in response.

Anna could feel her face flush with heat. Out of the corner of her eyes, the walls seemed to tilt down on her, as if the entire room could collapse. A tingling sensation spread quickly over her entire body. These were familiar predecessors to a full-blown panic attack. Terror was only a few early symptoms away. She had to focus on something, anything, to avoid a further progression.

"I'm just saying that we can never resent you. We love you," her dad said.

Anna could feel her left eyelid twitching rhythmically, and sweat was dampening her forehead. The walls continued to dip down, dancing slowly and dramatically in her peripheral vision. She forced herself not to look at the bowing upper corners of the room, and instead distracted herself by staring at the old painting on the wall. She studied the thick brushstrokes of the landscape.

No matter what, she couldn't let her parents see what was happening. If she showed any outward expression of what she was feeling inside, any remaining hope to persuade them of her sanity would be gone.

"But, Anna," Mr. Yoder said, his voice cracking, "we are concerned about your health...and your sanity."

"You don't have to be concerned, Dad," Anna finally managed to say. She could feel heat all over her face, and she continued to study the painting hanging above her father's head. There were eighteen thick brushstrokes in the evergreen tree placed on the right side of the canvas.

"I'm sorry I wasn't forthcoming with you earlier. I was hoping you'd open up on your own," Mrs. Yoder said. "But your sister told us about last night."

"What about last night?" Anna said.

"She told us about the dinosaurs."

"What are you talking about?" Anna finally looked away from the painting and met her mother's eyes. "What did Sheila tell you?"

"She said you think the dinosaurs move at night," Mrs. Yoder said. She was still frowning.

"You know Sheila always exaggerates," Anna said quickly. She could hear her dad sigh loudly and shakily, the way he sighed when he was tearing up. She couldn't look at him. She stared at her mom.

"Well, then, why don't you give us the unexaggerated version?" her mom said. "Did you see the dinosaur statues moving last night?"

"I saw something," Anna said. "It may have been my imagination, though."

"What about the caveman?" Mrs. Yoder asked. "Do you think the caveman moved himself into the middle of the road?"

"I don't know," Anna said. She couldn't allow herself to process this moment fully. She couldn't be here for this conversation. She'd have to mentally record it and replay it later, when she was in the privacy and safety of her bedroom. "I didn't see it happen."

"Exactly how long have you believed the statues move at night?" Mrs. Yoder said.

The heat and claustrophobia of the room intensified simultaneously. The question sounded so personal, Anna was tempted to tell her mother that it wasn't any of her business.

"I don't know for a fact that the statues are moving," Anna said. She quickly returned her gaze to the landscape painting and took a moment to carefully examine the thick evergreen brushstrokes before she continued. "I know what I saw. I'm just not sure if it was real or imagined."

"Okay," Mrs. Yoder said.

"I've got to go," Anna said impulsively. Without thinking, she stood up. She had to get out of this room. She looked down at her parents, who were now holding hands and looking up at her with wide eyes.

"Sit down, Anna," Mrs. Yoder said. "We need to have this discussion."

"Please," her dad said.

"Okay, but I'm supposed to meet someone online," Anna lied. She sat down, glanced at her parents, and then returned her gaze to the painting. "I need to get going."

Anna could hear her mom mumble something, and from the corner of her eye, she could see her arms folding across her chest.

"There will be plenty of time for you to get online," Mr. Yoder said. "But for now, we need to talk."

"Okay," Anna said. "So let's talk."

"You've always had such a gifted imagination," Mr. Yoder said. He chuckled softly to himself. "I remember the stories you used to tell when you were a little girl. Do you remember your imaginary friend that was a gorilla? You named her Gorgeous. Gorgeous Gorilla. You were always telling stories about her that were so convincing, I almost believed they were true."

Anna said nothing.

"But, honey," her father continued, "you're not a child anymore. You cannot allow your imagination to be your reality."

"I know, Dad," Anna said. "I understand that what I saw last night might have just been my imagination."

"You know logically that statues cannot move on their own," Mr. Yoder said. "How could you ever entertain the idea that seeing them move was anything other than your imagination?"

"Because I saw it," Anna said.

"What exactly did you see?" Mr. Yoder asked.

"Recently these sounds started waking me up at night," Anna said, purposefully ignoring her father's question in her hurry to present what she believed to be the most compelling evidence. "I could feel the whole house shake when they moved."

Anna looked at her mom and dad, both staring at her with a strange coldness.

"Anyone would have felt the shaking," Anna said. "It was like a little earthquake."

"It's funny that Sheila didn't mention it," Mrs. Yoder said. "She was here in the same house with you."

"Sheila is a heavy sleeper, but I bet if you guys were here, it would have woken you up."

"Do you think it was an earthquake?" Mr. Yoder said. "Or maybe some shock wave from an earthquake in California or something?"

"No, because it was preceded by that awful sound. Like a growling."

"A growling?" Mrs. Yoder said, shaking her head.

"I guess that doesn't sound like an earthquake, does it?" Mr. Yoder said.

"I've only heard it a couple of times," Anna said quietly. She felt a calm in her confession, but she could see the disbelief in her parents' eyes. "I'm not lying."

The roads from town to Shady Springs Dinosaur Park were unusually empty and lonely. Scenarios of what might transpire that evening in the Katz house ran though Sheila's head. If the Katz brothers told their mom that Sheila confronted them at the rec center that afternoon, it could make things a lot worse between the Yoder and Katz families. With the Katz family reputation in mind, the situation could go from simply cold to dangerously hostile.

The gravel loudly hit the undercarriage of Sheila's car and left a cloud of dust hanging in the air behind her, rendering the rearview mirror almost useless. By the time she neared the intersection of Park Street and Forest Hill Road, Sheila knew what she had to do. She turned up the road and drove toward the Katz home.

As her tires popped and crunched on the gravel driveway, Sheila stuck her head out the car window to watch the ground in front of her. The last thing she needed was to run over a beer bottle and blow a tire out right here on Katz property.

In the dim light of late afternoon, it looked as if the house was abandoned. The dirty curtains that hung in the front windows were set against the blackness of the interior of the house. If this were any house other than the Katz house, she would assume no one was home. But Mrs. Katz was surely hiding in the shadows. She had probably watched Sheila drive up the long road.

As Sheila parked the car and approached the house, she heard the front door pull open. Mrs. Katz was standing in the doorway, a cigarette dangling from her mouth. She wasn't smiling, waving, or motioning Sheila to walk up the front porch and enter her home. She was just watching, as if she had pulled open the front door only to get a better view.

"Good afternoon, Mrs. Katz," Sheila said as loudly and cheerfully as she could manage.

Mrs. Katz flinched, almost imperceptibly, then took her cigarette out of her mouth and let out a long, curling stream of smoke. "Hi, Sheila," she said. She was leaning against the doorway. The top three buttons on her yellow short-sleeved blouse were open, revealing the unadorned edge of a white bra. The yellow fabric of her blouse was noticeably darker under her arms, as sweat stains extended out nearly to the breast pockets. "Helluva day, isn't it?"

"It's a bit muggy," Sheila said, "but it's nice. Do you mind if I come in?"

"Sure," Mrs. Katz said loudly. Then she bowed slightly and made a long, sweeping gesture with her arm. "Come on in."

Mrs. Katz didn't move as Sheila brushed by her on the way into the house. She smelled strongly of whiskey, smoke, and body odor. If Mrs. Katz was tipsy, the conversation would be either much easier or much more difficult.

Sheila stepped into the living room, which was illuminated only by the dim light of the waning sun filtered first through the trees and then the half-closed curtains.

Sheila sat down in the armchair, and Mrs. Katz remained standing.

"Can I offer you a drink?" Mrs. Katz said.

"No, thanks, I'm fine."

"Mind if I have one?"

"Not at all."

Mrs. Katz disappeared out of the living room, and the sound of ice dropping in a glass could be heard. Sheila stared at the assortment of newspapers, mail, dirty dishes, and clothes lying on the floor. She noticed the apple bars lying on the floor next to the folding chair, right where Mrs. Katz had placed them during her last visit.

Mrs. Katz reemerged with a tall glass filled with ice and a brown liquid. Sheila wondered if she had already switched from mixing whiskey and Coke to just drinking the whiskey straight.

"Coke," Mrs. Katz said, raising the glass. "I love it."

"Very refreshing," Sheila said, playing along.

Mrs. Katz took one more long drag off her cigarette, then dropped it on the floor and stamped it out.

"What did you want to see me about?" Mrs. Katz sat clumsily on the couch. She didn't seem tipsy; she seemed drunk. Sheila considered if she should go ahead with her planned discussion.

"I wanted to let you know that I spoke with your boys today," Sheila blurted out before she could overthink it.

"Really?" Mrs. Katz said. She took a long drink of "Coke" and furrowed her brow at Sheila. "Where did you find them?"

"They were playing basketball at the rec center."

"Do you always hang out at the rec center, or were you out looking for my sons?"

"I was in town anyway for work."

"You're going to pull that armrest apart," Mrs. Katz said, pointing toward Sheila's right hand.

Sheila had unconsciously been playing with a loose string unraveling on the chair's armrest. She was surprised at how nervous she felt. "Sorry. Anyway, I ran into your boys at the rec center, and I spoke to them about the whole situation with the car accident."

"They don't need to be harassed by you, or anyone else," Mrs. Katz said. "Let the cops worry about that."

"I actually saw Tom at the bookstore," Sheila said. "He's the one that told me where to find Matt and Jeremy."

Mrs. Katz sat back in the sofa, gripping her drink tightly in both hands. She said nothing.

"I wanted to talk to Matt and Jeremy myself, to clear the air," Sheila said. "So I confronted them."

Sheila could see the frown on Mrs. Katz's face deepen, but she remained silent.

"Before Matt and Jeremy got home and told you that I confronted them, I wanted you to hear it from me," Sheila said.

"That wasn't fair of you to talk to them behind my back," Mrs. Katz said. "Were you hoping they would slip up and incriminate themselves?"

"Not at all," Sheila said. "I just wanted to hear their side of things."

"Well," Mrs. Katz said after finishing the last of her drink, "what did they tell you?"

"They said they knew they have a bad reputation, but they didn't have anything to do with moving that caveman."

"Of course," Mrs. Katz said. "And you think they are lying, right?"

"Actually," Sheila said. "I believe them."

Mrs. Katz's eyes opened wide, and she stared at Sheila for what felt like a full minute before responding.

"Thank you," she said. "I know my boys would never hurt your dad."

"I don't know if we'll ever really know what happened that morning," Sheila said.

"I'll let Jeremy and Matt know you are on their side on this one," Mrs. Katz said.

"Thanks," Sheila said, standing up. The living room had grown even darker over the course of their brief conversation, and she had to squint at the floor to avoid obstacles on the way to the door.

"I guess it is no secret who I believe is behind all of this," Mrs. Katz said.

Sheila turned and saw Mrs. Katz was still sitting on the couch, her face obscured in the darkness. "Who?" she asked.

"It's your sister," Mrs. Katz said. "I'm sure of it."

"We don't think you're lying," Anna's father said.

"But sometimes," Mrs. Yoder said, "people take action. They create situations to justify their own beliefs."

"What the hell does that mean?" Anna said. She couldn't believe she just swore at her mom. She couldn't believe she wasn't even going to apologize for swearing at her mom. The confrontation didn't seem real. The frowning woman didn't really seem like her mom, so it didn't matter what Anna said to her.

"I know you love your father dearly," Mrs. Yoder said, "and I know you would never intentionally hurt anybody, but is it possible that you may have moved the caveman?"

"What?" Anna couldn't believe it. Her stomach clenched with sickness. "Why would you ever accuse me of something like that? It's absurd."

"I think it is crazy too," her dad said quickly. "But Tom doesn't think the Katz brothers did it. And Anna, sweetheart, you were the only other person around for two miles."

"What about Mrs. Katz? I'm sure she was home," Anna said.

"Mrs. Katz? Anna, why on earth would she do that?" Mrs. Yoder said. "Think about what you are saying."

"Why on earth would you think that I did it?" Anna said. "Why don't you think about what *you* are saying?"

"I don't think you did it," Mr. Yoder said. "But Tom called here this afternoon. He was actually checking on you, but I talked to him a bit. He said he spoke to Matt and Jeremy, and he just wasn't convinced they had anything to do with moving that caveman."

"I thought Tom was a better policeman than that," Anna said. "Did it ever occur to Tom, and to everyone else, that those boys might be lying? And even if they didn't move the caveman, how can he assume it was me?"

"You were one of the only people around," Mr. Yoder said. "Like I said, I don't believe you had anything to do with it, Anna. I told Tom as much and told him that you were with me the entire time I was here."

"But she could have had it set up ahead of time and simply needed to push it onto the road," Mrs. Yoder said. "She could have run ahead of your truck, through the woods, the minute you left."

"This is ridiculous. How can I prove I didn't do something?" Anna was talking faster and faster. Words were coming out of her mouth before she could even think about them. "Tom is just pointing a finger at me because I seem like an easy target. But think about the time frame. You and I were talking the entire time you were here, Dad. Then you left and met the caveman on the road. How fast do you think I can run? There is no way I could have outrun your truck and moved that heavy statue out to the middle of the street in just a matter of minutes."

"That's true." Her father nodded eagerly and glanced at her mother. He seemed to have an "I told you so" look on his face. Her mother didn't seem to notice.

"So if I didn't do it," Anna said, "and if the Katz boys didn't do it, and Mrs. Katz didn't do it, then how did the statue move?"

"That's the question," Mrs. Yoder said. "What do you propose?"

"Isn't it obvious?" Anna asked. Her parents stared blankly at her. She sighed. She had no choice but to say it. "It moved the same way the *T. rex* moved."

"The *T. rex* hasn't moved in over fifty years," her dad said. He seemed a bit disheartened.

"It moved," Anna said. "I heard it, I felt it, and I saw it."

Anna's parents exchanged glances, but remained silent.

"You want concrete proof?" Anna said. "Go take a look at the dead grass on the foot of the *T. rex*."

"The dead grass proves nothing," Mrs. Yoder said. "There are patches of dead grass all over this property. Is that evidence that statues all over the park have moved? No, it's evidence that the resident of this property isn't taking care of the yard."

"It's Sheila," Anna said with sudden realization. "If it wasn't me, and it wasn't the Katz brothers, and the statues didn't move on their own…then it has to be Sheila."

"Why would your sister do that?" Mrs. Yoder said. "She wouldn't."

"She's trying to unravel me," Anna said. "She's trying to scare me into leaving Shady Springs. I know she is tired of all the energy you and Dad put into worrying about me. It all makes sense."

"How does that make any sense?" her dad asked.

"I knew there was something going on between Sheila and Tom," Anna continued, unable to stop her revelations from being spoken just as quickly as they came to her. "She must have convinced Tom that I was the likely cause of all of this. She must have moved the caveman, and she must have somehow moved the *T. rex* too."

"Anna, you're talking crazy," Mrs. Yoder said.

"Well," Anna said, knowing her mother was right, "what did you expect?"

Logizomechanophobia
Fear of computers.

CHAPTER 10

"You've got mail," Sheila said, walking into Anna's room.

"Thanks for knocking," Anna said, her voice muffled by the pillow.

"Why are you moping? Mom and Dad just want to help. They love you."

"I know," Anna said. "And I am trying to remind myself that, in your own twisted way, you are just trying to help too. But scaring me into leaving the park is not very therapeutic."

"I'm not scaring you." Sheila sat on Anna's bed.

Anna turned over and looked at her sister. She was holding a small cardboard box.

"You are scaring yourself," Sheila said. "Your phobias are getting worse. You need medical help."

"What's in the box?" Anna said. Now wasn't the time to accuse her sister. Besides, her parents had probably already told Sheila about her suspicions.

"It came in the mail," Sheila said and put the box on Anna's bed. "You didn't order more strange books, did you?"

"No. It's probably junk mail. Like a laundry detergent sample." Anna buried her head back in the pillows.

"I'm going to make dinner," Sheila said. Anna could feel her sister getting off the bed. "I hope you join us."

Anna heard the door close. She rolled over and looked at the box. It was an eight-inch cube. She was surprised when she saw it was a delivery from Big Box Discounts. She hadn't ordered anything from them, and she didn't think they sent out any sort of free samples or junk mail either.

Anna wasn't sure if she should open it. She nervously pressed her ear to one side of the box, as if she'd hear a ticking bomb. She heard nothing. She shook the box, and something light swished around inside.

Anna pushed her fingernail into the packing tape and ran it along the seam, popping the top of the box open.

Inside there was a receipt sitting on top of something. The receipt had printed on it: *Message to Recipient: Beware of the dinos. HAHA! –CrazyCorn90*. Anna's pulse began to race. She hastily lifted the receipt to view a small plush *Tyrannosaurus rex* smiling up at her.

Instantly, the sound of unearthly rumbling filled her ears. The panic and terror that she had been holding back all afternoon screeched into the forefront of her mind. Anna screamed.

"What the hell are you doing giving your name and address to Internet people, Anna?" Sheila said. She was sitting on Anna's bed. Anna was shaking and cold from the sweat sticking her T-shirt to her back.

"I didn't give anyone my address," Anna said. She knew she was speaking too loudly, but that sound was replaying in her mind, and she had to talk over it. The crushing sound, she knew, was only in her mind. She had been able to fight off a full-blown panic attack, but it felt as if she were still hanging on the verge. "Maybe I am just crazy."

"Oh, poor you," Sheila said. "So now that you have worried Mom and Dad sick, and now that you have exposed yourself to some Internet stalker, now you are going to play the 'I'm just crazy after all' card?"

"I'm so confused," Anna said. She looked up at her sister. Sheila's face softened a bit, and she put her hand on Anna's knee.

"I didn't mean to yell," Sheila said. "To be honest, I think I'm losing my mind too."

Anna laughed a bit, but mostly for her sister's benefit.

"I brought those apple bars to Mrs. Katz," Sheila said. "It was awkward for five minutes, and then we screamed at each other for five minutes. Basically, I ended up calling her family trash."

"Nice," Anna said, and this time she let out a genuine laugh.

"I saw the boys," Sheila said. "They looked so much older. So much sleazier than I remember."

"Did you confront them?"

"I did this afternoon."

The sisters sat in silence for a moment.

"What did they say?" Anna asked.

"They said they didn't do it," Sheila said.

"Naturally." Anna stared at the stuffed dinosaur in her hands. He didn't look menacing; he looked wide-eyed and innocent. A children's version of a dinosaur, with all the sharp edges softened into a Disney focus. "Why did you tell Mom and Dad about the dinosaurs?"

"Because I love you," Sheila said.

"Nice answer. You watch too many Lifetime movies."

"Shut up," Sheila said. "I mean it. I thought they should know how troubled you've been lately. Things have gotten worse, I can tell. You haven't been sleeping, I think you're losing more weight, and these panic attacks…"

Anna stuck her head under the pillow. *Panic attacks.* That was the term she despised, as if the words themselves could trigger an episode.

"Sorry," Sheila said.

But Anna knew she wasn't. She probably wanted Anna to freak out right now, when Mom and Dad were here to see what she had become.

"Anna, do you know who sent you the dinosaur in the mail?"

"I think so," Anna said.

"Who?"

"CrazyCorn90."

"What kind of name is that?" Sheila frowned at Anna.

"A screen name. I don't know what it means."

"What's his or her real name?"

"I don't know," Anna said. She felt a sickness in her stomach. "I never gave him my address. I don't know how this happened."

"Great, it's a guy? Did you tell him your name?" Sheila said.

"Only my first name." Anna was struggling to remember that night when they messaged each other for several hours. What did she say to him?

"Why did he send a dinosaur?" Sheila said.

"I told him about the park."

"Oh," Sheila said, nodding. "That's how he found you. How many old dinosaur parks do you think there are? Did he know you were from Iowa?"

"No," Anna said. "Oh, wait…yes, it's in my profile."

"Anna, you have to stop this computer stuff," Sheila said. "There are a lot of freaks out there that prey on women like you."

"Agoraphobic women who see cement dinosaurs move at night?" Anna said.

"Yeah," Sheila said, half smiling. "Women like you."

Was that some kind of joke? Anna typed. She was relieved to find the board consisted only of herself and CrazyCorn90.

Why, did you laugh? CrazyCorn90 responded.

No, Anna wrote back.

I thought it was cute, CrazyCorn90 wrote.

Anna didn't even know how to respond. She paused long enough that CrazyCorn90 wrote another message: *I thought you would like it.*

It was cute, I guess, Anna responded.

I sent it right before you told everyone about the dinosaurs moving, CrazyCorn90 wrote. *It was bad timing, I guess. You know snail mail.*

Anna accepted this for only a moment before she typed, *Then why did you send it with a note saying 'Beware of the Dinos'?*

It was a joke, CrazyCorn90 wrote.

How did you find my address? Anna wrote. There was no response for several seconds. Anna's fingers began to shake a bit. Her mind was attempting to replay every online conversation she had had with CrazyCorn90, trying to find the point where she had told him anything about where she lived.

You told me you lived in a dinosaur park in Shady Springs, CrazyCorn90 finally responded. *Google took care of the rest. It was easy to find the address online.*

Anna wasn't aware of how tense she had become until she felt her shoulders fall slightly with relief in reading CrazyCorn90's words.

I'm sorry, Anna wrote. *I've really been on edge lately.*

And a bit paranoid? CrazyCorn90 wrote.

Yes. Anna shot a quick glance at her bedroom door, which was open a few inches. She got up and soundlessly closed the door. She returned to her computer. *My parents think I moved the caveman to fulfill some psychological need to justify my hallucinations…or something.*

What? Sounds like Mom is into pop psychology, CrazyCorn90 wrote.

Actually, I think my sister may have planted that idea in their head.

Why would she do that?

She wants me locked up, Anna wrote, her eyes rapidly moving between the keyboard and the door. *She hates that I get attention, and she wants me gone.*

You realize that you know the truth, CrazyCorn90 wrote. *You are the only one that really knows what is going on.*

I do? Anna tried to suppress her fear as she wrote. But she could feel it growing inside of her, threatening to erupt. *What do you mean?*

You are the only person with all the pieces to this puzzle. You know those things are really moving. You know the police investigated, and it wasn't the neighborhood boys, CrazyCorn90 wrote.

Sheila may have moved the caveman, Anna typed. As soon as her response posted, she posted several lines of periods so the text would scroll up and eventually disappear off the page.

Easy with the punctuation marks, there, CrazyCorn90 wrote after Anna had finished. *Afraid your sister will walk in and see what you wrote? You really are paranoid. But you know your sister didn't move the caveman.*

If it wasn't her, and it wasn't the Katz brothers, Anna wrote, *who does that leave?*

Don't you mean "what" does that leave? CrazyCorn90 wrote.

A poltergeist? Anna wrote.

Something supernatural, CrazyCorn90 wrote. *You know there is something going on there, but no one believes you. Everyone just assumes you are crazy because you happen to have a few phobias. But phobias are just survival instincts in overdrive. It's not inherently crazy to have phobias.*

That's true, Anna wrote. She looked again toward the doorway. It would be just like her sister to bust in at an important time like this. *What can I do?*

You have to get someone else to see it too. They have to see it in person, not pictures or videos that they could accuse you of faking, CrazyCorn90 wrote. *It can't be someone in your family who has an agenda. It has to be someone neutral.*

OK..., Anna wrote.

The next time you hear those sounds, CrazyCorn90 wrote, *call the police. Don't look outside, and don't go outside. Just call the police. Let them see it for themselves.*

Anna agreed with CrazyCorn90 and logged out of the session. Sheila was such a snob to think that real friendships couldn't be developed online. It wasn't like Sheila was that popular. Aside from her work friends at the bookstore, she didn't have that large of a social circle. She'd probably never get married, not unless she moved out of Shady Springs. Of course, the same could be said for Anna. The difference was that it mattered to Sheila, but Anna didn't care if she died a lonely virgin spinster.

Anna logged in to her e-mail account— SuicideSue@rocketmail.com. It was easiest to keep her login names the same. She saw four spam e-mails were in her bulk mail folder. It seemed that advertisers were the only people who ever sent Anna e-mails, so she often read them before deleting them. This time, however, she had an e-mail that appeared to be a real e-mail from someone named Kathryn. Anna smiled and opened the e-mail with the subject line: *Your Immediate Attention Needed.*

Dear Anna Yoder,
As the administrator of the Agoraphobics Support Circle, part of the larger Net Support Network, it is my duty to inform you that your account(s) is in violation of our Terms of Use agreement.

Only two account names are permitted per household. According to our records, five accounts have registered with matching IP addresses: SuicideSue; AmazingGrace1976; TomFriday; KTMaa; and CrazyCorn90.

If you feel this message has reached you in error, or if you access the Agoraphobics Support Circle from a public computer, please respond immediately with this information. Otherwise, please terminate three accounts within the next 30 days, or your IP address will be banned, and you will no longer have access to our support boards.

Thank you for your prompt attention to this matter.

Sincerely,
Kathryn McGillicuddy
Administrator
Net Support Network

Anna stared at the e-mail. She searched for any clue that this may be a prank. A sign that someone was out to make her feel like she was crazy. The e-mail address, the content of the e-mail, everything seemed real. Just as real as the cement dinosaurs that had lived in Shady Springs for the last sixty years. It suddenly seemed entirely possible that Anna was simply crazy.

<u>Hylophobia</u>
Fear of forests.

CHAPTER 11

"Mom, what is the risk of making a phone call to Dr. Fergus?" Sheila asked. She could already feel herself losing patience.

"I've given it a lot of thought, and I'm thinking that he will just make her more upset," Mrs. Yoder said. She continued to wash the long-since-clean coffeepot and stared out the kitchen window. "I wish I could understand why she is so certain. How can she be convinced that something that large and immobile is moving?"

"I don't know." Sheila looked out the kitchen window and saw the dim outline of the *T. rex* in the early evening light.

"And you're sure that you didn't hear any noises or feel anything like a small earthquake the other night?" Mr. Yoder asked. He was sitting at the kitchen table, awkwardly resting his cast arm at the table's edge. "You've never heard any strange sounds in the middle of the night?"

"No," Sheila said. "Of course not." She said this with as much certainty as she could. She was always a heavy sleeper, and slow to wake up. She only remembered waking up disoriented and then hearing Anna scream.

"So what if she had heard something?" Mrs. Yoder said, still staring out the kitchen window. "What would that prove?"

"Maybe if there was a small earthquake, or some strange noise, it could trigger a hallucination. It would be understandable, especially in the middle of the night," Mr. Yoder said. "Anna has always had a very active imagination."

"Overactive," Sheila said.

"Sometimes, yes, an overactive imagination. But if the noise was real," Mr. Yoder said, "her mind could easily fill in some blanks. She could convince herself that something fantastic was happening. It doesn't make her crazy; it just makes her creative."

Sheila took the coffeepot out of her mom's hands and placed it back in the coffeemaker. "I think Anna is making both of you crazy," she said.

"Shhh." Mrs. Yoder looked out the doorway, through the living room, and toward the closed bedroom door. "She might hear you."

"We can't keep living like this," Sheila said. "Call Dr. Fergus."

"Why?" Mrs. Yoder said, still whispering. "Why call him today or even this week? Let Anna cool off a bit, and then maybe she'll want us to call."

"Or maybe we won't need to call at all," Mr. Yoder said quietly.

"God, you guys," Sheila said, "I'm sick of everyone tiptoeing around this. Anna is mentally unstable. She needs professional help. She deserves professional help. She's getting worse and will continue to get worse."

"She seemed okay last week," Mr. Yoder said. "Before the accident, I mean."

"A grown woman who refuses to leave the property she grew up on, who refuses to eat even though she is underweight, that seemed 'okay' last week?" Sheila said, her voice growing in pitch and intensity.

"I meant she seemed stable," Mr. Yoder said, looking down at his cast.

Sheila felt sudden guilt for raising her voice to her broken father.

"I meant she seemed like herself," Mr. Yoder continued. "Even if being herself meant being a little different."

"That's so sweet," Mrs. Yoder said and ended her vigil at the kitchen window to sit across from her husband at the table. "Anna's always been your girl. No matter what."

"This is maddening," Sheila said. She could feel her voice shaking. She pulled a third chair up to the kitchen table. She had to say things carefully to not offend her parents, just as they seemed to say things so carefully as to not upset Anna. The family seemed to be held together by small talk and painfully careful word choices. "She is seeing things that are not there. She is hearing sounds that do not exist. Her social circle consists of Internet chat rooms with other sick people. She has no friends. She has no one but us. We have to get her some professional help. It's criminal to let her keep living like this and ruling over our family with her sickness."

Sheila carefully watched the expressions on her parents' faces. Her mother had her head tilted, and almost seemed to be slowly nodding. But her mother almost always nodded when listening to people. She probably believed it conveyed empathy, but it was often confused with agreement. Her father stared at the floor, his face unreadable.

"Let's give it a week," Mrs. Yoder said, reaching out and patting Sheila's hand.

"My God!" Sheila shouted and stood up. "What does it take to get a rise out of you people? I thought you guys were finally on board with getting some help for Anna. Now you want to give it another week?"

"Sheila, I'm sure you don't mean to take that tone," Mrs. Yoder said. "We're all just under a lot of stress."

"That's damn right we're all under a lot of stress," Sheila said. "Because we are all living with a five-hundred-pound gorilla in the corner and pretending she isn't there. That's tough to do. What sort of a wake-up call do you need?"

"We are awake," Mr. Yoder said.

"Oh really?" Sheila said. "Your daughter thinks the dinosaurs are moving at night. She may have moved a statue out in front of your car, which could have killed you. You think she's okay. You coddle her and tell her that she's just a sensitive girl. Well, I think you are the sick ones—almost as sick as Anna!"

"Stop, Sheila," Mrs. Yoder said. "Your father and I are well aware that something is going on here. We just don't yet know what that something is."

"Well, I can save you some time and tell you what that something is: your youngest daughter has completely lost touch with reality and is a danger to herself and to us." Sheila couldn't contain the anger in her voice, and if she stayed any longer, she may do something regretful. She just knew that Anna was sitting in her bedroom right now, with the door shut, on the computer. She could almost hear the rapid clicking of the keyboard. She was probably telling the chat room crazies that her sister was an evil bitch who was trying to turn her own parents against her. Sheila lowered her voice and said, "Anna will destroy this family. She has complete control over us."

"No, she doesn't," Mrs. Yoder said.

"Oh yeah?" Sheila kept her voice low. "Who determines what we can have on the table at Thanksgiving because of her 'food issues'? Who forced the major financial decision for you guys to keep this house long after the rest of us moved out, even though she doesn't pay for anything? Who dictates that we can't all leave town at the same time so that we can deliver groceries to this place and check on her? Who wakes us up the middle of the night? Who is the center of almost every family argument?"

"Okay, Sheila," Mr. Yoder said, "we get it. We know Anna requires a lot of time and attention. But she doesn't *make* us do anything. We love her, and we choose to do things that help her. We take care of her because we are family."

Sheila stared at her father. He looked so fragile and sincere. It was understandable where he was coming from, but at the same time, his naïveté was making her want to reach out and shake him.

"Who is the only logical suspect for putting you in the hospital?" Sheila said. "How about you ask Tom for his list of suspects?"

"I spoke with Tom this afternoon," Mr. Yoder said. "She may be under suspicion, but let's not use the ugly word 'suspect.'"

"Anna may have serious problems," Mrs. Yoder said, "but she isn't a criminal. She would never intentionally hurt her father."

"That's it. I gotta go," Sheila said, walking toward the front door. "The dysfunction is suffocating me. I need some air."

The air was humid and thick with gnats. As Sheila walked through the park and toward the woods, she kept her head down. She stared at her feet and tried to focus on placing one foot in front of the other. Maybe Tom could convince her parents that they needed to have Anna committed.

As Sheila walked into the woods, she suddenly sensed someone was behind her. She quickly turned and saw the landscape of the Shady Springs Dinosaur Park. The statues were glowing softly in the light of the setting sun. Scanning the park, she saw no movement.

Her parents were still inside the house, probably talking about how humid it was, or how great this new coffee tasted, or anything other than the fact that their eldest daughter had just stormed out in anger over their inaction regarding their mentally ill youngest daughter.

Sheila continued to walk through the woods. She wasn't really sure of where she was going, but she knew every tree within a two-mile radius of her childhood home. She would often walk in these woods after family fights—which used to involve boys or chores or allowance money. Now the fights seemed to center only around Anna.

Sheila froze. She heard someone behind her once again. She took a few slow steps forward, listening carefully. Maybe she was just getting spooked by her own footsteps on the twigs and rocks underfoot. She heard nothing unexpected, but she could feel a chill go through her. Something was out there.

Sheila leaned against a tree, just so she could feel some protection on her back, as she scanned the woods. She wasn't too far from the house. She could still see the *T. rex* looking impressively large against the backdrop of their small home. The other dinosaurs and cavemen spotted the landscape. As she stared at them in the distance, they almost seemed to ripple and sway. She knew it was an optical illusion—a product of the distance, the heat, and her own nerves. But it was a disturbing observation. Perhaps this is what Anna was seeing. But to her, it was real.

Looking around the woods, Sheila could see nothing. A squirrel ran up a tree a few yards away, birds could be heard and seen all around her, but nothing unexpected or out of the ordinary. The woods were, as always, dark and familiar. Except for that feeling that something or someone was out there. It was a real and almost tangible feeling in the air—it was a new feeling. She wasn't alone, as she usually was on these walks.

Suddenly, Sheila felt the tree shudder behind her. She quickly jumped forward, away from the tree, and turned around. She expected to see someone's hands reach around the tree, shaking it. She cautiously looked around the thick trunk. There were no hands. She listened for the sound of the Katz brothers snickering, but she heard nothing. No one was there.

"Just the wind," Sheila said, looking doubtfully toward the top of the tree. Leaves rippled in the light breeze. Every now and then one would escape from the canopy and flutter gently to the ground. It was either her imagination or it was the wind. It was more reassuring to assume it was the wind.

Sheila wasn't going to allow herself to get spooked out of a therapeutic walk. Just as she began to step forward to continue her stroll, the ground seemed to move slightly underfoot. It was the sensation of stepping off an automatic walkway at the airport and onto solid ground. The underfoot sensation of movement was simply different, and a little dizzying. Sheila froze. Maybe it was low blood sugar. Maybe she was just hungry. If she hadn't spent so much time in that inane conversation with Mom and Dad, maybe she could have had something to eat.

Sheila looked around, now unsure if the feeling of someone watching her was just paranoia or if she really had company. Although she wanted to believe she was without an audience, she put on a show of bravery and walked with false casualness and confidence for several yards.

Then the ground seemed to jolt slightly, and a low, almost inaudible, rumble could be heard. Sheila surprised herself with her own scream and began running. As she ran, she knew she could hear and sense someone following her. She pumped her legs quickly, afraid that if she lost momentum, whatever was in the woods with her would catch up.

She reached the edge of the woods and ran through the dinosaur park. She ran around the statues, trying to stay at the greatest distance possible from each of them. Someone could be hiding behind them. She couldn't look at any of the statues. What if they *were* moving? What if that was the sound? What if that was what caused the ground to shake? Anna could be right. What if something supernatural was happening here? None of her thoughts made sense, but they came to her too fast to censor—so each one felt real and plausible.

Sheila reached the house, swung open the door, then quickly locked it shut behind her.

"Sheila? Is that you?" It was her mother's voice. "Are you okay?"

"I'm not sure yet," Sheila said, trying to catch her breath. Looking out the small windows that lined the front door, she saw the *T. rex* standing as it always stood. The park was still. The only movement that could be seen was the gentle swaying of the trees in the late summer breeze.

Sheila turned and saw her mom standing behind her. She looked tired. "You're not sure if you're okay?" Mrs. Yoder said.

"I'll be fine," Sheila said. She lied. She hated lying and making things seem okay when they weren't. It was especially hypocritical given their recent argument, but she didn't want to tell her mom and dad that something was out there. "Don't worry, Mom."

<u>Lygophobia</u>
Fear of darkness.

CHAPTER 12

Anna pressed her ear to the wall. She could hear her sister on the phone in the master bedroom next door. She sounded upset.

"I didn't see anyone," Sheila's muffled voice said. "Can't you just come and check it out?"

There was a pause. Anna pressed even harder, her ear crushing painfully against the cool wall. She strained to hear what sounded like a whisper break the silence.

"Anna is in the next room," Sheila's voice said quietly.

Anna felt her cheeks flush. She wanted to run into the kitchen and pick up the other phone and scream, *"Stop talking about me!"* but Mom and Dad were still in the kitchen, as far as she knew. Plus, if Sheila was talking to Dr. Fergus, that would pretty well seal her fate of being carted off to the mental institution.

"Something is out there," Anna heard Sheila say. She pulled away from the wall and sat on her bed. Had Sheila really said that? It was so hard to trust anything now. Her mind had allowed her to have conversations with imaginary online friends, even allowed her to order and mail herself a package without ever remembering doing so. Had Sheila really said that she saw something outside, or was this more of her mind trying to keep up the facade?

The thought that Anna kept trying to hide was that it now seemed possible that she somehow moved the caveman in the path of her father's car. The more she tried to ignore that thought, the more she became obsessed with it. Maybe she had watched for him. She knew what time he always came. Maybe as soon as his truck drove around the corner toward the house, Anna had pushed the caveman into the road, then ran back through the woods to greet her father at the house. No one had thought of that before. Everyone thought Anna ran and pushed the caveman onto the road after her father left, which seemed absurd. But this revelation seemed possible. It even seemed likely.

There was a light knock on the bedroom door, startling Anna from her thoughts.

"What?" Anna said. She looked around the room, suddenly self-conscious that she was just sitting at the edge of her bed doing nothing. It looked weird. She reached over and grabbed the alarm clock and began to play with the buttons.

"Can I come in?" Sheila's voice was on the other side of the door.

"Yes," Anna said.

When Sheila walked into the room, she almost didn't look like Anna's sister. She was pale. Her eyes looked dark and afraid. Maybe she was afraid of Anna. Maybe she somehow knew Anna had moved the caveman.

"Can we talk for a minute?" Sheila said.

"What's going on?" Anna said, setting the alarm clock back on the bed stand.

"I need for you to be completely honest with me," Sheila said, sitting on the bed next to Anna. "What, exactly, do you hear at night?"

Anna looked closely at her sister. Was she kidding? Was she setting her up? Was this a prerequisite interview before Anna could be sent to the crazy house?

"You told me there was no sound," Anna said. "You told me it was all in my mind."

"Just tell me what you think you heard," Sheila said. Her eyes darted nervously toward the closed door and then back at Anna.

"Since when do you care about the products of my overactive imagination?" Anna said.

"I think you may have heard something real," Sheila said in a low whisper.

"Please don't mess with me, Sheila."

"I'm not. I'm not saying that your imagination hasn't been at play here, magnifying the situation."

"Did you hear something too?" Anna asked. She braced herself physically, pulling her feet up onto the bed, grabbing her knees and pulling them up to her chest. Anna feared the warm tingling she felt on her cheeks would suddenly spread to the rest of her body and she'd lose control before she could even find out what her sister was trying to tell her.

"I don't know exactly what I heard," Sheila said, "but I heard something and felt something too. It felt like there was someone out there in the woods."

"Who?" Anna said.

"I don't know. I'm not even sure there was anyone out there."

"But there was *something* out there," Anna whispered, hugging her knees tighter.

"Yeah," Sheila said. "I don't want to tell Mom and Dad until I figure out what is going on. I can't even begin to put my finger on this yet."

"Have you considered the possibility that I'm right?" Anna said. "The dinosaurs are moving."

"That doesn't make any sense, Anna."

"These sounds don't make any sense. The earth shaking doesn't make any sense. What I've seen with my own eyes doesn't make any sense."

"I know," Sheila said. She reached out and gently stroked Anna's hair. It felt awkward and uncomfortable, like a stranger giving an unsolicited hug. "Nothing makes sense. But I know there has to be a reason for all of this."

"Have you ever heard of a poltergeist?" Anna said.

"Girls!" There was a knock on the bedroom door, and the sound of their mother's voice. "Dinner is ready."

"Thanks, Mom," Sheila called. Then she turned back to Anna. "Not a word of this to Mom and Dad. I don't want them to think we are both crazy."

Anna's eyes popped open in the dark bedroom. She quickly scanned the room, but couldn't make out anything other than darkness and her glowing alarm clock. It read 3:29 a.m. Anna listened carefully, straining to hear any indication of sound that may have woken her up. All she could hear was the gentle whirr of the fan in her parents' bedroom next door combined with the jagged snores of her father. Perhaps his snoring had woken her up.

Anna turned to lie on her side. As she did so, the bed trembled a bit under her weight. Then it continued to tremble. Anna's heart began to beat faster. Was the earth moving, or was it just her bed? She felt her pulse in her temples, as if her veins were threatening to explode at the very possibility that the giant cement statues were moving once again tonight.

Surely the trembling bed was her imagination. Just like her imagination created online accounts and tricked her brain into believing she was talking to someone other than herself. Just like her mind was probably blocking out the fact that she had laid a deadly trap for her own father.

The trembling of the bed suddenly stopped. A very low, unnatural growl, graveled and unholy, filled the air. It was subtle, but Anna could hear it. It wasn't loud enough to wake anyone, but it was there and just as real as the whirring of the fan.

Anna sat up in bed, her eyes staring into the blackness. The low growl sounded both near and far away, as if its source were far away, but the resulting sound was right there, like a voice from beyond this realm picked up by radio tuners.

Another sound was added to the first—this one slightly louder, but still a low rumble. Anna slowly swung her legs around and placed her feet on the floor. She could feel a vibration on the floor that tickled her toes. Anna stood up and walked toward the bedroom door. The sound of her father snoring grew louder. She wondered if she should wake him up. But what if she woke her parents and they heard nothing? What if they confirmed this was all in her mind?

Anna walked toward the living room. The rumbling sound grew and became more rhythmic. *Like giant footsteps.* Anna could feel a tingling all over her body, and she wasn't sure if it was the vibrations or if it was a panic attack rising inside of her.

Anna walked to the kitchen and picked up the phone. She cautiously looked out the window, afraid that what she might see could literally scare her to death.

She saw great shadows on the lawn. They were trembling. They were moving.

Anna quickly stepped back from the window, her hand shaking as she dialed 911, then dropped the phone on the kitchen floor. She felt the tingling take over her body, and she felt herself spiraling into a panic attack. If she screamed, she'd die. If she looked outside again, she'd die.

Anna picked up the phone and heard the operator on the other end, but it didn't sound like she was even speaking to Anna. It was as if she were in another dimension, completely disjointed. Everything around her looked disjointed. Slightly deviated from reality, but still reality. Anna felt her heart pounding fiercely inside her chest, and she knew she was about to die. This time she was really going to die. She shouldn't have looked out that window.

"Yes, even the fire truck came."

Anna could hear Sheila's voice before she opened her eyes. She didn't know where she was, but hearing her sister's voice was reassuring.

"Sheila," Anna whispered, holding her eyes shut. She had to be sure she was in a safe place before she moved or looked around.

"I'm here," her sister's voice said as Anna felt a slight warm breeze rush over her body. She imagined her sister leaning over her, and she felt her arm being patted. "I'm right here, Anna."

"Where are we?" Anna opened her eyes, squinting at a dim and hazy version of her sister before opening her eyes fully. She was on the floor.

"You're on the floor," Sheila said.

"Thanks, that's really helpful," Anna said and began to sit herself up.

"Whoa, careful." Sheila, who was kneeling next to Anna on the floor, reached down to Anna and gently pushed her head back down. "Let yourself wake up a bit before you try to stand up."

"I think I'm okay." Anna was lost in a moment of tenderness with her sister, but was suddenly jolted when she remembered what had precipitated her attack. "Those sounds. Did you hear the sounds?"

Sheila glanced over her shoulder before returning her gaze to Anna. Her voice lowered to a whisper. "I heard something. I don't know what I heard. But I heard something."

Anna's stomach tightened. She glanced around and realized she was lying on the kitchen floor. A pillow had been placed behind her head, and a light blanket covered her legs. She could hear people talking quietly in the living room, but Sheila and Anna were alone in the kitchen.

"Did you feel it? The earth was shaking." Anna watched her sister's eyes widen a bit, then look toward the living room again.

"I don't think I felt it," Sheila said. She looked very afraid. "I was too scared to move. I don't really remember anything other than waking up to a strange growling sound. Then I heard you screaming."

"Tell them," Anna said. "Please. So they don't think it's just in my head."

"Anna." Mrs. Yoder's voice interrupted. "I'm glad to see you are awake, dear." She knelt on the kitchen floor next to Anna. As she did so, Sheila quickly stood up and walked away. Seeing her sister so anxious made Anna even more nervous. It was as if she wasn't telling her something.

"How are you feeling?" her mom said as she touched Anna's forehead with the back of her hand. It was a gesture she had done since Anna was very young. It used to be how her mom gauged Anna and Sheila's temperatures when they were sick, but it had evolved into a touch of concern and love. In this moment, however, it felt as if her mom was attempting to measure Anna's sanity with the back of her hand.

"I'm sorry I'm so much trouble, Mom," Anna said.

"Have you moved your neck yet?" Mrs. Yoder said, seeming to ignore Anna's apology. "The paramedics didn't think it was broken, but thought you could have strained or sprained it…or something."

"You called paramedics?" Anna said. She sat up slightly, resting on the back of her elbows.

"No, *you* called the paramedics and the sheriff." Mrs. Yoder looked at Anna in a way that was neither amused nor sympathetic. It was annoyed. "We had to convince them to not take you to the hospital."

"I don't really remember what happened," Anna said. But she did. Somehow those cement dinosaurs were animated. The entire family could be in danger if she didn't play her cards right. "Can I ask you a random question?"

"What is it, sweetheart?" her mom said sweetly, but looked apprehensive.

"Do you believe in the supernatural?" Anna said. She immediately wished she hadn't. "I mean, I was having a really weird dream when I passed out, that's all. I'm just curious what you think about—"

"Oh, stop it, Anna." Mrs. Yoder was clearly attempting to sound playful, even lightly swatting at Anna when she said this. But the look of concern could not be concealed. She looked so worried and fearful. "Do you feel ready to stand up? You can join us in the living room."

"Us? Don't tell me the paramedics are still here," Anna said. She let her mother help lift her off the floor and onto her feet even though she felt strong enough to do it herself.

"No, they left a while ago," Mrs. Yoder said. "But Tom is still here."

When they walked into the living room, the room fell silent. Sheila and Tom were sitting on the couch and stopped their apparently private conversation to look up at Anna. Her father looked up from his magazine that he was reading on the easy chair.

"I'm sorry, everyone," Anna said. "Sheila, can I speak with you privately?"

Sheila looked at Tom, who nodded and stood up.

"How are you feeling, Anna?" Tom asked.

"What is this?" Anna peered around Tom's shoulder and at her sister, who was still sitting on the couch, wide-eyed and fidgeting. "With all due respect, I asked to speak with Sheila. Not you, Tom."

"Do you want to tell me what happened?" Tom asked.

"I passed out," Anna said, sighing.

"Tell me what happened before you passed out," Tom said. He smiled a bit, and it looked condescending to Anna.

"I didn't commit a crime, so why are you interrogating me?" Anna was surprised by her own boldness. She looked over Tom's shoulder again. "Sheila, could I please speak to you privately?"

Tom turned around and looked at Sheila. Anna noticed her mother and father were looking anxiously at Sheila as well. What was the problem? Tom nodded toward Sheila and must have whispered and mouthed something to her, because she nodded back and mouthed, "I know."

"Sure, Anna," Sheila said, standing up. "Let's go to your room."

Anna followed her sister back to her bedroom as no one in the living room said a word. As soon as Anna walked into the bedroom, she shut the door behind her.

"What the hell is wrong with you? What's wrong with everyone?" Anna whispered loudly at Sheila.

"Everyone is just worried," Sheila said. She sat down on the bed. She noticed Sheila's hands were shaking a bit, and her neck was a bit red.

"Why are you so nervous?" Anna asked. "And why aren't you telling them that you heard the sounds too?"

"Anna, they want to commit you," Sheila said.

"What?" Anna collapsed into the office chair, which squeaked loudly beneath her.

"It wasn't my idea," Sheila said quietly.

"Okay." Anna didn't even know if she believed her sister. But she wanted to. "I don't know what to say."

"I'm sorry," Sheila said. "Mom and Dad are worried that you are a danger to yourself and—"

"And to others?" Anna stared at her sister.

"I didn't say that."

"Well, I think that was clearly where you were going." Anna spun around in her chair and stared at the dark screen of her computer. Her reflection was distorted like a fun-house mirror. Like the way her family probably thought Anna saw the world. They really thought she was crazy enough to commit? Wasn't that for catatonic schizophrenics?

"There is a place up about ninety miles from here that can help you," Sheila said.

"Ninety miles…" Anna repeated. Her world had become so small that the idea of going ninety miles out into orbit seemed suicidal. Her skin began to tingle in that terribly familiar way.

"It has a great reputation," Sheila said, "a beautiful campus."

"Beautiful campus, great reputation," Anna said. "What are you, a recruiter? It sounds like I'm going to college."

"I guess it is sort of like getting an education," Sheila said with a small, insincere-sounding laugh.

"Why aren't they committing you too?" Anna looked at the reflection of her sister behind her on the monitor. Sheila had her head in her hands.

"Why would they?" Sheila said.

"Because you've heard it too," Anna said. "You know there is something going on out here."

Sheila said nothing.

"But you won't tell them that, will you?" Anna said. She turned around in her chair to see her sister with her face buried in her hands.

"The fact is that you need help," Sheila said, looking up. Her face was splotchy and red. "Mom and Dad are finally on board with getting you some help, and I don't want to ruin this opportunity for you by telling them that I heard some odd noises last night."

"How noble of you," Anna said.

"Your episodes are happening more often, you refuse to eat even though you are way too thin, and—"

"Okay, so that's the 'I'm a danger to myself' part," Anna said. "Now tell me again how I am a danger to others?"

"I never said you were a danger to others," Sheila said. "I was going to say you are a danger to yourself and you scare me."

"I scare you?" Anna laughed hoarsely. "How could I scare you?"

"I think you may be moving the statues," Sheila said.

Anna could feel her heart begin to race, but she couldn't put any words together. Did Sheila somehow know that Anna moved the caveman statue in the exit pathway of her father's pickup right before his visit? She stared at her sister for several moments before speaking.

"What does that mean?" Anna said.

"It's just a feeling, just a theory," Sheila said. "And it scares me."

"How could I possibly move the statues? How could I be strong enough to move a cement caveman?"

"I'm not just talking about the caveman. I'm talking about all the statues."

Anna could feel her jaw drop as she stared at her sister. Sheila fidgeted with her beaded bracelet for a few moments before continuing.

"I don't know exactly how you are moving them. I just know that you are."

"Okay, you *know* that I am," Anna said, suddenly aware that her voice had elevated to a near-shouting level. "So now you know for a fact that I am moving the statues. It really isn't a theory, then, is it? You've stated it as fact. No wonder Mom and Dad want to lock me up."

"I didn't tell them my theory," Sheila said, her voice quiet.

"Really?"

"I never said anything to them about it. They want to commit you because they can no longer care for you. They are afraid for you. Your panic attacks, your agoraphobia, your 'episodes,' the fact that you don't eat. You are self-destructing, and that is reason enough to have you get professional help."

Anna stared at her sister for a few moments that felt like hours. Finally, she leaned back in the chair, causing it to squeak loudly. "When are they taking me?" she said.

"They were planning to take you tomorrow morning."

"By police escort?"

"Tom showed up because of the nine-one-one call," Sheila said. She audibly sighed. "He stayed because he is a friend and he cares about you."

"So you think when I leave," Anna said, "the noises will stop and the dinosaurs will stop moving."

"Frankly, that's exactly what I think," Sheila said.

Anna stood up and opened the bedroom door. The low conversation in the living room froze as she walked out of the bedroom.

"Anna, wait," Sheila said behind her.

Anna could hear the springs on her bed squeak as her sister must have been standing up to follow her. She ignored Sheila and walked into the living room

"Now that everyone is here," Anna said to her parents and Tom, "let's take a look outside."

Eicophobia
Fear of home surroundings.

CHAPTER 13

Sheila couldn't bring herself to say the one word to Anna that was most on the tip of her tongue: telekinesis. She had read some articles online and in the bookstore on the subject, and Anna sounded like the perfect vessel for such powers. She had never believed in such things before now.

"Why do you want to go outside, Anna?" Sheila said. In the back of her mind, she couldn't help but wonder if it was a trap.

"I'm being committed. Can't you humor me?" Anna said coldly.

Sheila looked at her mom and dad. They looked worried, and much older than they had looked four days ago.

"Oh, honey"—Mrs. Yoder reached out to Anna—"I wish Sheila hadn't told you. I wanted to talk to you about it first."

Sheila watched her mother and Anna hug in a way that could best be described as perfunctory. They didn't mean it—there was no kindness or support in the embrace. Then they both looked at Sheila with coldness in their eyes. This was the Yoder family, in all its glory.

"Okay, Anna"—her father joined Anna and her mother, placing his hands on both their shoulders—"we can go outside to have a look if it will put your mind at ease."

"Anna, are you sure you want to go outside now?" Sheila said. "It's still dark."

"I've got my flashlight," Tom said. "We'll be just fine."

As the family walked out the front door one by one, Sheila watched. Everyone was still catering to Anna. They were bowing down to her psychosis, answering her every whim. Maybe they felt guilty arranging a bed for Anna in the mental hospital. Maybe, even more likely, Anna's charms as the delicate sick girl had bullied them all into submission.

"Aren't you coming?" Tom said as he followed the family, led by Anna, out the front door.

"Of course," Sheila said. "We wouldn't want to upset Anna."

Tom gave Sheila an odd look, but held the door open for her as she walked into the warm summer night.

The light from the house seeped out into the dinosaur park a few yards before the darkness overcame it. Sheila looked up and saw no stars or any sign of the moon in the sky.

"It's really overcast tonight," Sheila said to Tom, but he was walking quickly past her, and then past her parents, and didn't respond. He put his hand on Anna's back, and Sheila watched them both slow their pace and bow their heads down in conversation.

"Where are we going?" Sheila said loudly. Her parents turned around, and Tom and Anna were still in conversation. "What are we doing out here?"

"Can't you just be patient?" Mrs. Yoder said. "For Anna?"

"Everything's for Anna," Sheila muttered, but she intentionally said it loud enough to be heard.

"This is very therapeutic for her," Mrs. Yoder said.

"Oh, right, because you are an expert?" Sheila said. "Why are we sending her to the hospital? She could get all the help she needs right here."

"Stop it!" Anna yelled.

Sheila was suddenly aware of how loudly she had been talking. "I'm sorry," she said. She wasn't sure if she really felt bad, or just embarrassed.

"God, you think I can't hear you?" Anna said. As she walked closer to her parents, Sheila could tell she was shaking. "I'm crazy, not deaf."

Mr. Yoder let out a little chuckle, but immediately bit his lip. Everyone was silent for a moment, and a distant rumble of thunder could be heard.

"Why are we out here, Anna?" Sheila said. The way Anna was shaking looked unhealthy. Not like she was cold, but like she was so overwhelmed with feeling and emotion that her body couldn't handle it. Her mind was probably swirling with negative energy. Sheila suddenly felt very afraid to be outside with her sister.

"I would think that you'd be just as curious as me to see if the *T. rex* has moved," Anna said.

Tom gently patted Anna's back and smiled at her. This caused in unexpectedly hostile reaction to boil out of Sheila.

"We shouldn't be out here," Sheila said slowly, trying to hold back. She didn't want to anger Anna, but she had to warn her family. "I'm going inside before it starts raining, and I suggest you do the same. This isn't a safe or healthy exercise."

Sheila spun on her heel and walked toward the house. No one tried to stop her as she opened the front door and closed it behind her. Sheila listened carefully to the voices outside, but couldn't make out what they were saying. She waited a few moments in the tiny foyer of the house for someone to follow her inside. No one came. They all had to support poor little Anna, not even realizing what they may be dealing with.

Sheila kicked off her shoes and headed toward Anna's bedroom. Still shaking with emotion, she suddenly became aware of a vibration underfoot. Was she walking heavy-footed? The vibration was subtle, almost oddly soothing. There was a light tingling sensation, as if her feet were just about to fall asleep.

By the time she reached Anna's room, the tingling stopped. Rather than being reassured that nothing was happening, it only made the sensation more real in retrospect. Sheila forced herself not to dwell on it as she turned on Anna's computer.

Sheila bent over the desk, as if sitting in the chair would be an invasion of privacy but standing would keep a respectful distance. She opened the Internet browser.

Without even thinking of what she was looking for, but knowing she would find something compelling, Sheila opened the browser history.

Scanning the Web sites, she saw several visits to an e-mail account, a site called Net Support Network, a couple online bookstores, Google, and several other sites that weren't too surprising. Then Sheila's eyes landed on a Web site that made a chill go through her body.

Sheila paused and listened carefully to ensure everyone was still outside. She stood upright and walked over to the door. Peering into the hallway, she confirmed the house was still dim and quiet. Sheila returned to the computer and clicked on the Web site called Supernatural Energy in the Real World.

A poorly crafted Web site opened. It looked like it had been constructed using a free template. The background was a sickly green color. The name of the Web site was across the front of the page, a brief paragraph that Sheila skimmed over, and then several links. The links were in a large font that had the appearance of dripping dark green slime. They were: Spiritual Energy, Ghosts, Orbs, Poltergeists, Psychics, and Telekinesis.

Sheila moved the pointer to Telekinesis, but before she could even click on it, she heard a scream. She jerked upright and the mouse flew off the desk and dangled by the cord, inches from the floor. There was another scream. It came from outside. It sounded like Anna. She had to force herself to move and run down the hallway, toward the danger she imagined outside.

Running in the darkness outside, Sheila could see Tom's flashlight pointing to her father, who was crouched on the ground. She passed the *T. rex* in the darkness and couldn't help but nervously crane her neck skyward as she ran by. The head of the statue loomed high in the air, looking black and featureless.

As Sheila neared her father, she could hear Anna crying.

"Are you okay, Dad?" Sheila called as she neared the group.

"I'm fine," her father said. He turned and looked toward Anna, who was crying into her mother's shoulder. "Really, I'm just fine."

"What happened?" Sheila said. As she reached her father, she could see he was using his handkerchief to blot blood off his foot.

"I shouldn't have worn my sandals outside at night," Mr. Yoder said with a small chuckle. He put his handkerchief in the pocket of his jeans and struggled to stand up from his kneeling position.

"With your arm in a cast, I don't think you should be walking around here at night at all," Sheila said.

"It's okay, Anna," Tom said. He walked over and patted Anna on her back.

Sheila felt sick to her stomach. "Why is Anna upset?"

"Don't talk about me like I'm not here," Anna said. She looked at Sheila with her eyes full of tears. "Open your eyes."

"Sorry," Sheila said.

"No, Sheila," Anna said, "open your eyes. Can't you see what Dad walked into?"

Sheila looked at the ground next to her father. One of the smallest statues in Shady Springs was by his feet. It was the statue of a baby *Ankylosaurus*. He was about two feet high and three feet long, four feet if you included the extra foot of tail. It was lying on its side. There were cement blocks connected to its feet that were covered in dirt.

"Shrimpy?" Sheila said, recalling the nickname she and her sister had given the statue when they were kids. "Come on, Anna. Running into Shrimpy is nothing new. I think everyone in our family has stubbed our toe or bruised a shinbone on this little guy more than once."

"That's true," Mr. Yoder said. "But he is a bit misplaced. Obviously, we usually keep him planted in the ground."

Sheila squinted into the darkness, trying to assess exactly where they were standing in the park. Tom shifted the spotlight of his flashlight to a spot behind the group, further away from the house.

"What are you pointing at?" Sheila said. "I don't see anything."

"It's the holes where Shrimpy used to be," Anna said. "They don't look dug up. It's as if he jumped out of the position he had been in for decades."

"Are you sure?" Sheila asked. She could feel her stomach clenching. The air outside suddenly felt cooler, as if a storm might suddenly burst through the sky. The hairs on her arm were standing on end.

"Someone may have lifted him straight out, but it does look a little strange," Tom said. He panned his flashlight two feet from the patch of dirt, revealing the larger *Ankylosaurus*. The twenty-foot-long mother, who had always stood next to her baby, stood alone. Next to her were four holes. The holes were spaced apart into the shape of a rectangle. Each hole was tidy, it looked as if no dirt had been displaced. "I don't think I could have lifted that statue out so neatly if I tried."

"Now do you all believe me?" Anna said, her voice shaking. "The dinosaurs are moving."

Suddenly, Mr. Yoder was back on the ground.

"Dad," Sheila gasped and ran toward him. He wasn't breathing.

Enissophobia

Fear of having committed an unpardonable sin.

CHAPTER 14

The word "manslaughter" has a way of standing out, even in the most indistinct conversations. Anna pressed her ear to the door and listened to Sheila and her mother talking quietly on the couch. She was lying in bed, alone, as she had remained for the past week, when she thought she heard that word float into her ear. She couldn't be sure if it was real or imagined, but it jolted her out of bed.

"This can't be happening," her mother said. Anna could clearly hear the pain in her voice. She felt at once compelled to run out of her bedroom and into the living room to embrace her mother, and at the same time she wanted to hide in her closet, surrounded by boxes labeled "winter clothes" and "old toys." She wanted to do anything to be surrounded by the past instead of the present.

Sheila's words were more difficult to decipher through the door. They sounded like a quiet and sighing hum, sometimes jumping in pitch and then trailing off.

"I know you are right," Anna's mother said. There was a long pause, followed by a creak in the sofa springs. Anna imagined they were embracing, but she stood back from the door just in case one of them stood up and was walking down the hallway to check on her. They hadn't checked on her all day, although the constant anticipation of them checking on her was enough to keep Anna off the computer and off those supernatural Web sites all week. After she heard the hum of her sister's voice once again, she pressed her ear to the door once more.

Everything had happened so suddenly. One moment, Dad was standing and talking, and the next he was dead. It was as if the evil that hung in the air of the park had finally worked its way into his brain and switched off the light. The hospital said it was a blood clot that had broken loose and caused a severe stroke. They said it could have happened at any time. They didn't mention Dad frequently forgetting to take his blood thinner medicine as a cause, even though Anna's mom had mentioned this fact with great remorse several times. Everyone knew the blood clot had been caused by the accident.

All discussion of committing Anna had disappeared seven days ago, at the moment of her father's death. Anna imagined, however, that her family still intended to do so once the period of shock and mourning passed.

Anna heard her mom say her sister's name at the end of a long and undecipherable speech.

"Anna knows it," Sheila said clearly, followed by more indistinct humming.

Anna backed away from the door once more and sat down on her bed. "I do know it," she whispered. If Dad died as a result of the accident, and everyone thought Anna moved the caveman that caused Dad's accident, then Anna was the cause of her father's death. Anna hadn't imagined that word. She did hear them say "manslaughter."

"She's accusing me of manslaughter," Anna said slowly and quietly, as if saying the words aloud would help her to make sense of them.

Anna lay down in the bed. The mattress conformed warmly around her body like a protective embrace. For the first time, Anna wished she'd hear that terrible, unearthly rumble. She wished the *T. rex* would come crashing through the living room as unquestionable proof that the statues were moving themselves. It would be proof of Anna's sanity and innocence in one dramatic moment.

The bedroom felt impossibly large, and Anna felt impossibly small. The absence of her father, which was a dull ache that she had chosen not to tend to in the past week, suddenly felt horrific and glaring. As Anna cried, her sobs echoed off the walls of the empty room. Neither Sheila nor her mother came to check on her. Anna cried alone.

Sheila hadn't been able to steady her hands since Dad died. It was as if she were constantly shaking. Even when she wasn't crying, even when she thought she was in control, her hands were shaking. It was a strange and sad palsy that she could only hope would dissipate with time. She placed her hand on top of her mother's hands, which seemed to have a steadying effect and also comfort her mother at the same time.

Anna hadn't come out of her room even once to comfort their mother. She hadn't offered to cook or clean. She hadn't helped with arrangements for tomorrow's funeral. She hadn't spoken to a single one of the constant stream of guests who had come and gone from the house in the past week.

"Your dad loved that painting," Mrs. Yoder said. Her eyes stared toward the starving artist painting that hung on the wall. "I always hated it. That's why I didn't take it with us to the new house."

Sheila didn't say anything. She sat back on the couch and looked at the painting. She had never given it much consideration. It had always been there, ever since she could remember, anyway. It was as much a part of the house as the brick exterior or the windows. It blended in as part of the architecture.

"Was that wrong of me?" Mrs. Yoder asked quietly. She was still looking at the painting. "Do you think I should have moved the painting into the new house?"

"It's fine, Mom," Sheila said. "It's not a big deal."

"Maybe it was a big deal, and maybe it wasn't," Mrs. Yoder said. "I wouldn't know. I don't know if Jim would have told me if it were a big deal."

"It's not a big deal. I can promise you that. I never once heard Dad mention it," Sheila said again. She searched her mind for a new topic, anything to change the direction of the conversation. But she had nothing.

"I am worried that maybe it was a big deal," Mrs. Yoder said. "When we bought the new house, he packed this painting. He had it carefully wrapped it in bubble wrap and masking tape as it if had some value. I saw him carrying it out of the house, and I asked what it was. When he told me, I told him to turn around and hang it back up."

"And he did," Sheila said. "If it were a big deal, he wouldn't have hung the painting back up."

Mrs. Yoder's glassy eyes finally left the painting and looked at Sheila. "You know your father better than that. More than anything, he wanted to make us happy. I asked him to bring it back into this house and hang it up, and he did. I was hoping that when we sold this house, we'd sell that painting right along with it. I told him our small retirement house wouldn't be large enough for it. He didn't say a word. But he looked so disappointed. I'm worried this painting was a big deal to him, and I made him leave it behind."

Sheila rubbed her hand over her mother's back. "You guys shouldn't even have two houses to begin with," she said. "You should have sold this house like you planned and forced Anna to move into her own place."

Mrs. Yoder's eyes crinkled at the corners slightly when Sheila said this. Almost as quickly as the words came out, she immediately realized it was the wrong thing to say and the wrong time to say it. She looked back at the painting on the wall, studying the thick globs of paint that represented a green landscape at dawn.

"The painting looks good in this house. I'm sure Dad didn't mind leaving it here."

<u>Necrophobia</u>

Fear of dead things or things associated with death.

CHAPTER 15

Her father's ashes were in a carved wooden urn, sitting on top of a folding table with an ivory tablecloth. The cloth flapped in the wind, sounding like a bird taking flight.

The funeral was held in the backyard. The dinosaur park was just out of eyesight, blocked by the house, but the gray rounded top of the *T. rex*'s head could be seen just over the roof from where Anna was sitting. It was difficult to escape the *T. rex*.

Anna sat on the metal folding chair next to her mother. Mrs. Yoder must have known Anna was worried, and she had whispered to her that morning that her father wanted his funeral to be held here at the old house. Anna couldn't imagine her parents ever having a conversation about their future funerals. She knew it was a lie. They were holding it here at the house so they wouldn't have to have a fight over getting Anna to leave the house to attend her father's funeral.

With her peripheral vision, she could see Sheila peering around their mother and glaring at Anna throughout the service. Anna never looked up. She didn't want to see the look on Sheila's face. She didn't want to see anybody's face.

Anna wore her red beaded bracelet to her father's funeral. It was a symbol of self-control. She bought the bracelet online several years ago, from an eating disorders Web site, a *pro*-eating disorders Web site. The red bracelet was supposed to be a symbol of "bony pride." Anna thought it was pretty, and connected to the meaning—although she would never tell anyone that. It seemed so juvenile, especially since the young woman she bought the bracelet from was only seventeen. She stared at the red beads, barely processing any words coming from the pastor.

At the end, people formed a line to both her mother and the urn. People said things to Anna, but she didn't hear. She just watched the sparkle of the sunlight on her bracelet.

The line of people shuffled slowly by Anna, her mother, and her sister. They were like an exhibit at a zoo. People whispered to them in low and soothing tones as if they were wild animals that may unexpectedly lash out if anyone made any sudden moves.

Pastor Phil got on one knee in front of Anna. Anna felt embarrassed and wished he'd just stand up and walk away.

"Anna," Pastor Phil said, "I'm so sorry for your loss. Your father is in a place that is more wonderful than we can ever understand in this lifetime. He's with Jesus, Anna, and he feels no pain."

He used her name as if he knew her. He used her name twice, which made Anna cringe. It was a forced and false familiarity. Anna didn't know Pastor Phil. She had never seen him before this week. When she was a little girl and went to the Shady Springs Community Bible Church, Pastor John was the minister. He was a nice older gentleman with short silver sideburns and a mostly bald head. He never would have gotten down on one knee to talk to someone.

"Thanks," Anna managed to whisper. This seemed to satisfy the pastor, and he stood up and walked away. The line behind him shuffled forward. A few people seemed inspired by Pastor Phil's posture in front of the grieving, and they, too, took a knee in front of Anna's mother. No one else spoke directly to Anna, although many gently patted her shoulder as they shuffled by.

Tom, Pastor Phil, and Pastor Phil's overly perky wife, Mandy, stayed to help clean up after others had left. The folding chairs clanged loudly as they were collected two or three at a time. Tom and Pastor Phil would disappear around the house with an armful of chairs, and then Anna could hear the loud metallic clatter of the chairs being loaded into the bed of someone's truck. Eventually, there were only three folding chairs left to collect—and the Yoder women occupied all three of them. They sat in the vacant backyard, huddled close together in front of the wooden urn. No one said anything, or even moved, for what seemed like an hour. The sunlight began to dim before Anna realized how much time must have passed.

"Whenever you are ready," Pastor Phil said, his voice gentle with a practiced empathy, "I can place the urn in its box."

"Pastor Phil?" Mrs. Yoder's voice cracked. Anna looked at her, but immediately had to look away. The pain in her mother's face was too overwhelming to see.

"Yes, my dear," Pastor Phil said. He got down on one knee in front of Anna's mother. If he didn't look so sad, it would have appeared as if he were about to propose to her.

"I don't think I should have had Jim cremated," Mrs. Yoder whispered. "I think I made a mistake."

"I'm sure Mr. Yoder would be pleased with how you have managed his earthly remains," Pastor Phil said.

"He never told me how he wanted to be buried," Mrs. Yoder said, her voice gasping between tearful starts and stops. "I never even thought to ask him."

Sheila swung her arm around her mother, almost smacking Anna in the face. Her mother leaned away from Anna and cried loudly onto Sheila's shoulder. Pastor Phil placed one large hand on her mother's knee and held it there. His head was bowed, as if in prayer. Anna forced herself to do what she thought she should do. She touched her mother's left hand, which was lying motionless in her lap. Mrs. Yoder retracted her fingers ever so slightly. Almost imperceptibly. But Anna noticed.

The kitchen was filled with Tupperware containers and casserole dishes covered with tinfoil. Anna hadn't expected that everyone would show up to the funeral with a dish. Maybe mourning made some people hungry. She wondered how they would ever figure out which casserole's dish belonged to which person. Mandy, a pretty woman with a square jaw and curly short brown hair, brought two casserole dishes and insisted on hugging Anna not once but twice. The more her mom broke down crying, the more energy Mandy appeared to have. She was never at a loss for what to say, and her words seemed more prepared than spontaneous. Anna wondered if she had married the pastor just so she could go to a lot of funerals.

In the dim light, Anna could see out the kitchen window that only three cars remained at the house: Sheila's, Pastor Phil's pickup with folding chairs stacked in the bed, and Tom's police car. The dinosaurs were motionless, almost as if they were refusing to move at a time when anyone other than Anna might see them. Even the *T. rex*, which seemed to always have some motion if Anna watched carefully enough, was completely still.

Quiet voices, indistinct, could be heard from the living room. Anna wondered if they were talking about her involvement in her father's death. She listened for several minutes as she stood in the kitchen. Many random and inconsequential words could be deciphered, such as "whichever," "Jim," "happening," "sorry," and "food." Then the word "Fergus" came distinctly out of her mother's mouth. They were talking about Dr. Fergus, which could only mean they were talking about Anna.

Anna's instincts were to continue to stay in the kitchen alone, but she felt compelled to walk into the living room. She wanted to see what they would say to her face.

Before she could think about it any further, Anna walked quickly into the living room. The low murmurs of quiet conversation suddenly stopped. Sheila and her mother were sitting on the couch in the living room, and a rosy-cheeked Mandy was wedged in between them. Tom and Pastor Phil were drinking coffee and sitting in two recliners facing the couch. All five faces were looking at Anna.

"Hi, Anna," Mandy said brightly. "Come and join us."

Sheila furrowed her brow and glanced over her shoulder, toward the hallway.

"Did you think I was in my room, Sheila?" Anna asked.

Sheila didn't move, she just stared at her sister. "I didn't know where you were," she said, but her cheeks were flushed as if she had been caught in a lie.

"Were you talking about Dr. Fergus?" Anna asked.

No one said anything. Not even Mandy.

"Yes," Mrs. Yoder said finally. "I mentioned that I didn't see him at the service today, but he sent a beautiful flower wreath."

"How nice," Anna said. She tried to force a smile, but she could feel the sides of her lips twitching uncontrollably as they refused to curve upward.

"It really is beautiful," Mandy said quickly. "It's the one with the white and blue flowers sitting by the mantel."

"That was thoughtful," Anna said. Sheila was looking at Tom, who was looking at his coffee mug. "I'm going to go lay down."

Psychophobia
Fear of the mind.

CHAPTER 16

"Are you staying with your mother tonight?" Tom asked.

Sheila wished Tom would grab her hand as she walked next to him down the long gravel driveway to his police car. Instead, he stared forward as they walked.

"I'll stay with Mom," Sheila said. "Someone has to be responsible."

"What about Anna?"

Sheila missed a step and nearly tripped as they were walking. She cringed at the mention of her sister's name, and she felt guilty for this involuntary reaction, but couldn't possibly repress it.

"What about her?" Sheila said.

"Who is staying with Anna?" Tom stopped walking and turned to look at Sheila for the first time since she had begun escorting him to his car. His face softened when their eyes met. "I mean, are you guys staying here?"

"Yes," Sheila said.

"I'll check on you all tomorrow morning," Tom said, opening the car door.

"Do you think Anna did it?" Sheila blurted out. The words came out faster than she could stop them.

"Well…" Tom sighed loudly. He closed the door to his car without getting in. He squinted at Sheila as if he were really considering the question. "My personal opinions aren't necessarily the official opinions of the department."

"What is your personal opinion?"

"I think there is something very strange happening here," Tom said, looking Sheila in the eye. Then he shook his head and opened the door to his cruiser once again. "Something very strange indeed."

"What does that mean?" Sheila said. But Tom was already pulling his car into the driveway and backing it out onto the dirt road. He gave her a nod of good-bye as his car drove past. Sheila called after him, "What the hell does that mean?"

Sheila watched as the police car drove down the dirt road, kicking up enough dirt and dust to cloak the car in an ethereal cloud just before it turned out of sight. She suddenly had the uncomfortable feeling of being watched. She turned, but there wasn't anyone in the driveway or by the house. The only ones watching, through painted eyes, were the dinosaurs.

"You're being stupid," Sheila whispered to herself as she quickly walked up the driveway and pulled open the front door.

Anna's fingers moved faster than her mind could think. Without even the slightest pause in the rapid percussion of keystrokes, her eyes moved quickly back and forth between the computer screen and her closed bedroom door.

You need to do a test, CrazyCorn90 wrote.

Anna knew CrazyCorn90 wasn't real, but she had become so dependent on her online friends that she had nowhere else to turn.

What kind of test? Anna wrote.

See if you can move some something. Something small, was CrazyCorn90's response.

Anna looked around her immediate surroundings. A pen was lying beside her computer.

How about a pen? Anna wrote. *How do I do this?*

Clear your mind. Then focus all your energy on the pen.

OK, hold on.

Anna got up from her chair and quickly poked her head out her bedroom door. Seeing and hearing no one nearby, she quietly closed the door and returned to her chair. She took five slow and deliberate breaths. Then she stared at the pen. She imagined herself moving the pen with her mind.

She continued to stare, trying to will the pen to move, until she realized she was holding her breath and needed to gasp for air.

The pen isn't moving, Anna wrote.

You have to believe you can do it, or it won't work, CrazyCorn90 replied.

What, like Tinkerbell? I have to "believe" for it to exist? Anna wrote. *This is silly.*

You have to believe it, and you have to fear it, CrazyCorn90 wrote. *That's a powerful combination for a mind like yours.*

"I can move this pen," Anna said out loud. She stared at the pen, envisioning it moving, repeating in her mind the phrase, *I can move this pen.* Nothing happened.

It's not moving, Anna wrote.

Trust me, you can move it. Try to get upset or scared, CrazyCorn90 replied. *You need that energy.*

I don't know if I can force myself to get scared.

Sure you can. You get panic attacks so easily. Just think about getting a panic attack.

No, that isn't working.

OK, well, I didn't want to do this, CrazyCorn90 wrote.

Anna frowned.

But you don't understand what I am, CrazyCorn90 continued. *I am not sure you are even capable of understanding what I am.*

If you are trying to scare me, you are succeeding, Anna wrote. *But I'm not going to have a panic attack.*

You killed your father, CrazyCorn90 wrote. *There is a dark place in your mind that knows this is true. You caused the car accident that led to his death. You killed your dad, Anna.*

The words began to run together on the screen, and Anna felt that familiar tingle of panic. It started in her cheeks and threatened to envelop her entire head and then body. Anna tried to refocus on the computer screen.

Move the pen now.

Anna stared at the pen. Her palms sweat as she clenched her fists in concentration. She could feel her entire body shaking. Was it true that she had moved the caveman? Had she really killed her father? A scream was pressing to get out of her mouth, and she held her lips closed tight to contain it. She knew she could move the pen, and the implication of doing so was terrifying.

There was a slight quiver. Then the pen rolled about an inch from its starting point to the edge of the desk and fell to the floor.

Sheila sat in her car, the air conditioner blowing her hair back and leaving her forehead almost icy cold. She held her cell phone in her hand and stared at the house she had grown up in. Before she could second-guess herself further, she flipped her phone open and began to scroll through her address book until she found "Fergus, Theodore." She clicked "OK."

"Dr. Fergus," a male voice answered.

"Hello, Dr. Fergus," Sheila said. "This is Sheila Yoder."

"Good to hear from you, Sheila," Dr. Fergus replied.

Sheila was surprised by the familiar tone of Dr. Fergus's voice. It was almost as if he were expecting her call. "I'm calling about my sister, " she said. "I'm very concerned for her, and I need your advice."

"Well, Anna and your family have been on my mind," Dr. Fergus said. "I'm sorry to hear about your father. How are you holding up?"

"I'm doing all right, I guess," Sheila said. "My parents were really close to committing Anna, and then my dad died. My mom hasn't been willing to pursue it since then, but I know that Anna will only continue to get worse."

"Worse how?" Dr. Fergus said.

"She isn't eating, she's paranoid, I don't think she's sleeping, she's hallucinating, and her panic attacks are getting more frequent." Sheila didn't want to tell Dr. Fergus that she believed Anna may somehow be responsible for the dinosaurs in the park moving.

"Your mother had expressed concern that my presence may actually send your sister into a panic," Dr. Fergus said. "I know she was planning to bring Anna into the hospital herself for that reason."

"She was," Sheila said. "But since Dad died, Mom told me she is no longer really pursuing help for Anna. I think it's just too much for her to deal with."

"Could you bring Anna to the hospital?"

"I don't see how. She might go on her own if Mom convinced her, but there is no way she'd go just because I want her to. I'd have to forcibly remove her from the house, and I don't think I'd be physically able. I also don't think I'd be emotionally able to do so."

"Could Tom help? Could he convince Anna to go to the hospital?"

"There is no way that Tom would do it without my mom asking him to."

"I can't say that I blame him for that."

"So what are my options?"

"I'll tell you what," Dr. Fergus said after a long pause. "I'm leaving town tomorrow, and I'll be gone for about a month. How about I give you a call when I get back, and we can arrange a meeting?"

"A month?" Sheila said with a sigh. "There is no way we can wait a month. I don't think we can even wait a week."

"Well…" Dr. Fergus paused as if he were weighing his options. "How about I swing by tonight? I wanted to be able to share my condolences in person with your mother anyway, if you don't think she is too exhausted from the funeral today."

"No," Sheila said quickly. "She has enjoyed all the company, I think."

"I'll see if I can't gently steer the conversation with your mother to the topic of Anna. If Anna is open to it, maybe I can talk to her too."

"That would be great."

"You may not want to mention my visit to Anna, just in case it would cause her to panic or even run away," Dr. Fergus said. "Besides, I'll probably just end up speaking with your mother, and there would be no need to upset Anna."

"Thank you," Sheila said.

Anna stared at the pen that had fallen to the floor for several moments. She took five long, slow breaths, and then she focused her thoughts on moving the pen. The pen twitched, as if pulled by an invisible string. Anna clasped her hand over her mouth, suppressing a cry. She turned back to the computer.

It moved. Does this mean I have telekinesis?

I think it shows how powerful your mind is, CrazyCorn90 wrote. *Have you ever heard of thoughtforms?*

Is that like telekinesis?

Not quite, but similar, I suppose. When your mind strongly believes something, it can manifest into reality.

Anna paused, trying to understand what was being said. Then she slowly typed, *Am I creating thoughtforms?*

You created me.

Anna leaned back in her chair. Her stomach tightened. She had accepted that she was somehow "typing for two" when she had online conversations with CrazyCorn90, or some of the other screen names in the Agoraphobics Support Circle. She was willing to believe that part of her mind was simply blocking out those additional keystrokes, giving her selective amnesia, to create the illusion of a conversation with another person. It had never occurred to her, however, that CrazyCorn90 might be a real manifested entity.

Where are you? Anna typed.

There is no simple answer to that, CrazyCorn90 responded. *The oversimplified and misleading answer is that I exist in your computer.*

Anna pushed herself away from the computer. She stared at the screen and the blinking cursor that awaited the next message. Anna stood up and walked to the other side of the room, pressing her back against the wall, her eyes never leaving the blinking cursor.

A *ding* startled Anna. She squinted at the screen. Surely this was a message from someone else, someone real, in the support group. The message read, *I am real because you made me real. I am a thoughtform.* It was from CrazyCorn90.

Anna ran up to the computer and turned off the monitor. She stared at the blackened screen, her own distorted reflection staring back. She then heard a loud *ding* as another message must have just posted. Anna quickly reached behind the computer and pulled out the power cable. Her bedroom was suddenly quiet as the constant whir of her computer was silenced.

Phronemophobia
Fear of thinking or thoughts.

CHAPTER 17

Anna pushed her peas around on her plate. Neither Sheila nor her mother had said anything the entire meal. They seemed to be exchanging a lot of glances, though, as if each expected the other was just about to speak.

"Thanks for dinner, Mom," Anna said.

"I think this is Mandy's casserole," Mrs. Yoder said. She gave Anna a small smile and then glanced back at Sheila. "Did you girls get enough to eat?"

Mrs. Yoder stood up, walked to the sink, and dropped the plate in. She stared out the kitchen window and toward the darkening orange sky.

"Plenty," Sheila said. "Why don't you go and lie down? I'll clean up."

"Thanks, sweetheart." Mrs. Yoder turned away from the window and walked out of the kitchen, placing her hand on Sheila's shoulder as she walked by.

"Is mom okay?" Anna asked.

Sheila rolled her eyes. "You just now noticed?"

Anna didn't say anything, but returned her attention to pushing peas around her plate, occasionally eating one at a time.

"No," Sheila said. "Mom isn't okay. Mom lost her husband, our father. She's mourning. She's broken. She's devastated. She's not okay."

"Sorry," Anna said.

"If you weren't so self-involved, you wouldn't ask such thing," Sheila said. Then she sighed. "Listen, I'm sorry. I didn't mean to snap."

"It's okay," Anna said. "I know Mom is having a rough time. We all miss Dad."

"Yeah." Sheila stood up and brought her plate to the kitchen sink.

"Sheila, I need to ask you something important," Anna said. "Have you ever heard of thoughtforms?"

"Thoughtforms?" Sheila said. She quickly dried her hands with the towel sitting next to the sink and sat at the table next to Anna. "Is that some kind of therapy?"

"No," Anna said. "It's when someone believes something so much that it actually becomes real."

"Like the power of positive thinking?" Sheila asked, squinting slightly.

"No," Anna said. "I mean when someone's thoughts are so powerful that they manifest themselves into something physical."

"Um…" Sheila lifted her eyebrows. She looked Anna up and down quickly, as if she wasn't sure what to say. "I have not heard of anything like that. Was that in the metaphysics book you ordered?"

"I don't think so," Anna said. "I read about it online."

"I wouldn't worry about it too much, Anna," Sheila said, standing up and returning to the sink. "You've got enough on your plate right now without scaring yourself over something that is obviously fictional."

"Sheila," Anna said, "I think the dinosaurs are alive. I think they are alive because of me."

The clatter of dishes falling in the sink jolted Anna. Sheila turned and looked at her with a strange look on her face.

"You can't be serious," Sheila said. Her face looked less doubtful, and more afraid. The expression on her sister's face made Anna even more nervous.

"I moved the caveman," Anna said. "I killed Dad."

Sheila's eyes widened. She quickly wiped her hands on her shorts and returned to the chair next to Anna.

"Don't say that, Anna," Sheila said. Her eyes looked damp, as if tears were beginning to well.

"I didn't do it on purpose," Anna said. "But I'm sure it was me."

"You aren't making any sense," Sheila said. She sniffled. "Maybe you should go and rest."

"All my life, I've had no fear greater than losing Dad," Anna said. "Dad was the only one in this family that ever loved me, and that I ever trusted. I was so afraid of losing him, that I killed him."

"What?" Sheila said, shaking her head.

"My fear killed him," Anna said. "I mean, I don't remember moving that statue. But I was so afraid of something happening to Dad, so convinced that something *would* happen to him, that I created a thoughtform. The thoughtform, *my* thoughtform, killed Dad."

"Are you saying that your fear made the caveman unearth itself and place itself in the middle of the road?" Sheila said. A tear streaked down her cheek.

It terrified Anna that Sheila might believe her. It was just more proof that it was real.

"Yes," Anna said. "And how do you think that baby *Ankylosaurus* moved?"

"Your thoughtform?"

"Yes. I don't know what the other dinosaurs are doing, but I do know that they are alive. They are alive because I gave them life."

"If you gave them life," Sheila said, "then you can take it back."

"I don't know how," Anna said. "I don't know if I can."

A knock at the front door made both Anna and Sheila jump in their chair.

"Don't freak out, Anna," Sheila said. "Please."

<u>Pantophobia</u>
Fear of everything.

CHAPTER 18

Anna stared at the landscape oil painting on the wall. She didn't want to look at Dr. Fergus. She hated the way he looked at her, not like he was looking at her, but like he was trying to look *in* her. Her mother and sister flanked her on both sides of the couch, perhaps as a show of support or perhaps to ensure that she wouldn't run. Dr. Fergus sat in the chair across from the couch, right under the painting. It was easy to stare at the painting and pretend that she was paying attention to Dr. Fergus.

"Can you do that, Anna?" Anna's mother squeezed her knee.

"Do what?" Anna asked, still staring at the picture. She was counting the thick brushstrokes in the evergreen tree.

"Tell Dr. Fergus about the sounds you've been hearing," her mother said. "Tell him about the dinosaurs."

Anna's gaze fell down, and her eyes met with those of the doctor. He was sitting with his legs crossed at the knees and his hands folded in his lap. His face was clean-shaven, his head full of brown and gray hair that was cut short but slightly frizzy on top. Deep lines defined his jowls and creased his forehead. He looked older than Anna remembered. Looking at him, and the way those small brown eyes of his looked at her, made Anna sick to her stomach. She quickly returned her gaze to the landscape painting.

"I'm sure you and Sheila have already told him all about that," Anna said.

"Please, Anna"—her mom squeezed her knee again as she said this—"just tell him in your own words. He can help you. He can help all of us."

"This isn't just about you, Anna," Dr. Fergus said. His voice was low and his words deliberate. The way he overenunciated things made Anna feel as if he were taking to a child. "We're just trying to create an open dialogue that can benefit your entire family. Everyone has been under a great deal of stress, and everyone is handling it in their own way. Why don't you tell us a bit about what you've been going through lately?"

There was a low and distinct growl.

"Did you hear that?" Anna said, turning quickly to look at her sister.

"No," Sheila said, slowly shaking her head.

"What did you hear, Anna?" Dr. Fergus said.

Anna didn't turn to look at him. Instead she stayed focused on her sister. "I heard the rumble," Anna whispered to Sheila. "You know the one."

Sheila's face twitched. She looked in Dr. Fergus's direction and let out a small and nervous-sounding laugh.

Then another growl sounded. This one louder. Anna could feel the floor beneath her feet vibrate. Sheila looked pale.

"You heard that, didn't you?" Anna said.

"Yes," Sheila said, her eyes wide.

"I heard that too," Anna's mom said. "Probably just thunder. I bet it's going to rain."

Anna looked out the small window in the living room. The sun was setting. A dark orange glow illuminated the tops of the trees in the distance. A few bright stars were already dotting the darkening sky. There were no clouds.

"Anna," Dr. Fergus said, "how have you been managing your anxiety during all the changes that have happened recently?"

"Changes?" Anna said. "You mean my dad's death?"

Suddenly a loud and unmistakable unearthly rumble filled the house. It was terrifying and inescapably loud. The floor vibrated and the entire house shook as if in an earthquake. The landscape oil painting swayed back and forth on its nail, at first gently and then violently.

Anna looked at her sister. Sheila grabbed Anna's arm and said something that Anna couldn't hear over the sound of the unnatural and unearthly roar. Anna turned to her mother, who was looking up at the ceiling, toward the ceiling fan, which was trembling and threatening to fall out of its base.

Anna stood up. Although both her sister and her mother held her arms, it was easy to pull away. She ran to the kitchen, stumbling and holding the wall as she went. She got to the kitchen sink, holding on tightly to the edge of the countertop, and looked out the window.

The outline of the *T. rex*, black against the early evening sky, could clearly be seen. It seemed closer to the house than ever before. Then, with a sudden movement that coincided with a distinct and gravelly growl, the *T. rex* lurched forward. Anna gasped and stepped back.

Then, just as suddenly as the sound had started, it stopped. Anna stared out the window, unable to move. She could hear her mother in the living room, asking Dr. Fergus if he was all right. Anna couldn't move. The *T. rex* was at least twenty feet closer to the house than it had been this morning. Perhaps even closer.

"Anna?" It was Sheila. She sounded like she was catching her breath. "Are you okay?"

"Look," Anna said. She could feel the warmth of her sister standing right behind her.

"Holy God," Sheila whispered. "They've all moved."

A chill went through Anna's body. She was so fixated on the *T. rex*, that she hadn't even noticed every dinosaur in park was now turned and facing the house. They were converging.

"I'm calling Tom," Sheila said.

Anna turned and walked past her sister and to the living room. There she saw Dr. Fergus sitting on the couch. He was touching his forehead and looking at his fingers as if looking for blood.

"The painting fell on Dr. Fergus," Mrs. Yoder said as she entered the living room from the hallway. She was holding cotton balls and a brown bottle of hydrogen peroxide in her hand.

Anna glanced at the wall where the landscape painting used to hang. There was a nail plus a rectangle of darker wood on the paneling, like a ghost of the painting. The painting was now lying faceup in the chair that Dr. Fergus had once sat in.

Sheila quickly brushed past Anna from the kitchen. "Let's get out of here, everyone," she said as she flipped her cell phone shut. "I don't think this is a safe place to be right now."

"What are you talking about?" Mrs. Yoder said. "It was just a small earthquake. It's over now."

"No, Mom," Sheila said. "It's not an earthquake."

A loud and nightmarish screech, followed by a low rumble, made everyone flinch and cover their ears at once. The floor began to shake violently.

"They're coming!" Anna screamed.

"Stop them!" Sheila screamed back. Her eyes were filled with tears.

"I can't," Anna said. "I don't know how."

Anna's mother and Dr. Fergus were both holding on tightly to the couch. They looked at Anna and her sister with a look of utter terror and confusion. Anna began to run toward the hallway and toward her room, but soon lost her balance and fell to her knees. She crawled down the hallway and into her bedroom.

Just as she plugged in her computer, the rumbling stopped. She could hear her mother crying in the living room, and Sheila was shouting for everyone to leave. Anna's computer chimed, indicating it was up and running. Anna quickly pulled up her Internet browser and went to the Agoraphobics Support Circle.

Help! Anna typed quickly. *Anyone here?*

Always. It was CrazyCorn90 who replied. *Trouble?*

How can I stop the dinosaurs? Anna wrote.

You can't kill a 900-ton cement dinosaur, I can tell you that, CrazyCorn90 responded.

A low rumble began to fill the air.

If my thoughts manifest into something real, why can't my own thoughts stop it? Anna wrote.

The computer began to shake.

"Anna!" Sheila ran in and grabbed Anna's arm. "Come on. We have to get out of here."

"Wait," Anna said. "I don't know how to stop the dinosaurs yet."

"You can't stay any longer." Sheila pulled on Anna's arm so hard that it hurt. The floor vibrated, and the low rumble evolved into a deep growl.

As Sheila pulled Anna away, she read a final message on the screen: *Take control. Remove their energy source.*

Anna ran behind Sheila through the living room and toward the front door. White flakes began to fall like snow. Then large chunks of white ceiling dropped to the floor all around them.

The low growl seemed even louder when they emerged outside. Sheila was running ahead of Anna, and Anna could see Dr. Fergus backing out of the driveway with her mother in the passenger's seat beside him. Her mom looked so frail and almost dreamlike through the haze of the windshield.

Sheila pulled open her car door, motioning Anna to hurry. As Anna ran, she looked to her right to see all the dinosaurs were converging on the house. A *Triceratops* was penetrating the kitchen window with a long cement horn. The *T. rex* was looming over the house. Their movements were awkward and heavy, bizarre and supernatural. Their joints had elasticity despite having the appearance of cement. All the dinosaurs walked on cement platforms, which had stabilized them when they were planted in the ground. Behind the dinosaurs, the field was empty and covered in holes of various sizes.

Simultaneously, the dinosaurs froze and then slowly craned their necks toward Anna. A long car horn sounded.

"Anna, run!" Sheila yelled.

"You go!" Anna yelled back, not taking her eyes off the *T. rex*. The *T. rex* lifted his head high as if sniffing the air.

"I'm not leaving without you!" Sheila screamed. "Come on!"

"No, go!" Anna screamed back, waving her arms at her sister. She turned and looked at Sheila and mouthed the words "go now." Sheila looked reluctant, but began to quickly back her car down the driveway.

Anna turned back toward the *T. rex*. All the dinosaurs were pivoting, turning to face Anna. The *T. rex* threw his head back. A strange, graveled roar filled the air.

"I don't believe any of you exist," Anna said. The rumbling grew louder. She took a deep breath and screamed, "None of you are real!"

The *Stegosaurus* was closer than any other dinosaur to Anna right now. It took slow and deliberate steps. Its tail, with three long spikes at the tip, swung from side to side as it walked.

"Stop!" Anna yelled. She could feel the familiar tingle in her cheeks. She knew she had to fight off the panic attack if she had any hope to survive. "None of you are alive."

Anna took a step backward. Her foot slipped on the gravel driveway, and she fell back, catching herself painfully on her elbows. The dinosaurs seemed to move faster toward her. As she scrambled to stand up, she was now just two feet away from the *Stegosaurus*, and the rest weren't far behind.

The dinosaurs had a peculiar odor of wet cement, paint, muddy earth, and something else that Anna couldn't work out. Something rotting and evil.

"I'm not afraid," Anna said quietly. She wasn't sure she believed it at first. Then she forced herself to take a small step forward, toward the *Stegosaurus*. The sound of growling and rumbling quieted, but the dinosaurs continued to move steadily toward her.

Suddenly, the *T. rex* bent over with an open maw, his teeth slick and white with fresh paint. His jaws snapped shut inches from Anna's face—creating a sickening wind that smelled of cement and rot.

The tingle in Anna's cheeks returned. She had to take control. Her fears and beliefs had created these horrible thoughtforms, so destroying her fears and changing her beliefs would surely end them. She had to believe that her fear was a choice. If she didn't believe that, then these things could destroy not only her, but everyone in Shady Springs and beyond.

Anna knew she had to take control. Her fear was a choice.

"I'm not afraid!" Anna screamed, her voice filling the air with an intensity that she didn't know she had. The tingle in her cheeks disappeared and was replaced with a sensation of a warm late summer breeze blowing in her face. "I'm not afraid."

The rumbling sound disappeared. The dinosaurs froze. Their faces once again seemed flat and painted. They didn't look real, alive, or dangerous. They were merely old statues from an old dinosaur park, nothing more. The smell of paint and rot still hung in the air, but as Anna stood and stared at the twenty large and small dinosaurs and two cavemen around her, that, too, dissipated.

Anna turned and began to walk down the gravel driveway, under the archway, and onto the dirt road. She left the convergence of dinosaur statues behind her, united and frozen in a hunt against a prey that had disappeared. As she rounded the corner, she saw her sister standing outside her car, waving her arm in the air. Further down the road, she could see a sheriff's car, with lights flashing, driving quickly toward them both.

"Anna!" her sister screamed, her voice cracking. She closed the car door and ran toward Anna.

"I'm okay," Anna said as Sheila squeezed her in a tight embrace. She could feel her sister trembling. "Don't be afraid."